NORTH

The Book

"A Social Justice Horror Story"

YVETTE KENDALL

www.stravardlux.com
Ph: (678) 661-9608

Science Fiction / Horror / Biblical Futurism / Fantasy

3780 Old Norcross Rd. #103
Duluth, Georgia 30096

First Edition, Fifth Print, February 2024

Printed in the United States of America

ISBN: 978-1-7371440-7-6 [Hardcover]

Visit www.StravardLux.com

Other IP Attachments

This book incorporates elements from the screenplay and teleplay of, "NORTH", created and authored by Yvette Kendall. This novelization, "NORTH, The Book" brings to life the captivating world and narrative envisioned in those scripts. While staying true to the core story and characters, this book offers readers a deeper exploration of the tale, providing additional insights and perspectives.

The creative work contained within these pages is a collaborative effort, with the original screenplay and teleplay serving as the foundation upon which this novel is built. It's a testament to the power of storytelling, allowing a single narrative to find expression through different mediums.

We hope you enjoy this literary adaptation of "NORTH," as it takes you on a unique and immersive journey through the imagination of Yvette Kendall.

Disclaimer

This disclaimer is provided to inform readers of the unique nature of the content within this science fiction/horror book. The subject of this book deals with "Social Justice Horror" and we want you to be prepared, and to establish certain expectations:

Fictional Content: This book is a work of fiction and should be treated as such. Any resemblance to actual events, places, or persons, living or dead, is purely coincidental. The characters, settings, and scenarios presented in this book are products of the author's imagination.

Horror and Dark Themes: This book contains elements of horror, suspense, and dark themes that may include graphic and disturbing content, violence, supernatural phenomena, and psychological distress. Reader discretion is advised, and this book may not be suitable for all audiences.

Suspension of Disbelief: Readers are encouraged to suspend their disbelief and immerse themselves in the fictional world created by the author. While the events and technology described may stretch the bounds of current scientific understanding, they are integral to the story's speculative nature.

Psychological Impact: The author acknowledges that horror and suspenseful content can have a profound psychological impact on readers. It is recommended that readers exercise self-care and consider their emotional well-being when engaging with such content.

Exploration of Fear: This book explores the genre of horror as a means to evoke fear, suspense, and intrigue. It may challenge readers' comfort zones and evoke thought-provoking questions about the nature of fear and the unknown.

Adult Content: This book may contain mature themes and content that is intended for adult readers. Reader discretion is advised, and it is not recommended for young or sensitive audiences.

Entertainment Purpose: The primary purpose of this book is to entertain and engage readers through imaginative storytelling. It is not intended as a source of factual information, scientific knowledge, or guidance on real-life situations.

Limited Liability: The author and publisher disclaim any liability for any adverse physical, emotional, or psychological reactions that may result from reading this book. Readers assume all risks associated with engaging with the content.

By reading this science fiction/horror book, you acknowledge and accept the content's fictional nature, its potential to elicit emotional reactions, and your responsibility for your own well-being while engaging with it. If you find the content disturbing or uncomfortable, it is advisable to discontinue reading. Your choice to read this book implies your understanding and acceptance of these terms.

Dedication

After writing my first science fiction novel, "*The GOD Maps: Volume One*," in 2018, truly, I thought that was it. I thought this was a strike of lightning that unearthed a rare seminal find in my mind. Then, in November of 2022, I was struck again with "*NORTH*." Now, it is as clear as day to me what my purpose on this Earth truly is. I dedicate this story to all Black people who have to fight to be seen, heard, and to live life openly and out loud. I dedicate this to our ancestors who had to innovate ways to just exist every day. One hundred years after The Great Migration began, we are still dying and going missing while traveling. I dedicate this to the souls that have been lost on any migration that WE have been a part of. I dedicate this to the millions of Black people who will never know exactly where we came from and can only plan for where we are going. I dedicate this to all the Black men, women, and children who are born with trauma in our blood that we can't seem to filter out. I dedicate this to the past, the present, and the future because WE ARE STILL HERE.

With boundless love and respect,

Yvette Kendall

Foreword

As I stand on the precipice of introducing you to the pages of this social justice horror thriller, a flood of emotions wells up within me. At 52 years old, I carry with me the echoes of my grandparents' stories—stories of resilience, hope, and the relentless pursuit of a better life during a time when the American landscape was fraught with challenges and barriers. Their migration from the oppressive South to the promise of the North, particularly in Chicago, laid the foundation for my own journey.

This book is, in many ways, a culmination of my life's experiences, a tribute to my ancestors, and a testament to the enduring legacy of the Great Migration. As a Black woman, I've witnessed the struggle for equality and social justice, and as a writer, I've channeled these experiences into the creation of a narrative that seeks to illuminate the darkest corners of our shared history.

The Great Migration was not just a physical journey; it was a voyage of the soul, a quest for freedom, dignity, and the right to live life on one's own terms. It was a movement that reshaped the cultural, social, and political fabric of America, and yet, the stories of those who embarked on this transformative journey are often untold or obscured.

In these pages, you will embark on a harrowing yet thrilling journey through the annals of history, where social justice meets the supernatural, and the horrors of discrimination and prejudice take on a tangible form. This tale weaves together the struggles of the past and the present, illuminating the timeless pursuit of justice and equality.

As an author, I strive to shed light on the complex and multifaceted issues that have shaped our society. I hope that this novel will not only entertain and captivate you but also ignite conversations about the enduring relevance of the Great Migration and the ongoing fight for social justice.

To those who came before us, whose sacrifices and determination paved the way, and to all who continue to stand up and speak out for justice, this book is for you. As we delve into the depths of this social justice horror thriller, may we remember our history, honor our ancestors, and forge a path forward toward a more equitable future.

Thank you for joining me on this journey.

With deep respect and gratitude,

Yvette Kendall

Table of Contents

"Every white person in this country—and I do not care what he or she says—knows one thing. They may not know, as they put it, "what I want," but they know they would not like to be black here. If they know that, then they know everything they need to know..."

~James Baldwin

CHAPTER ONE

Winston Gale drives down Peachtree Street in the Little Five Points area of Atlanta in a great mood. He has proposed to his longtime girlfriend, Lori, and he is stoked about the promotion he is up for at the magazine where he is one of the top writers. He is leaping from the life of a social columnist into the grainy world of investigative journalism full-time. As he drives, he notices that the beautiful, tree-lined streets that Georgia is known for, now bear a striking resemblance to a political battleground.

The landscape is changing into an outdoor market for an upcoming election. He watches as nefarious-looking individuals adorn light poles and mailboxes with posters, all bearing the words "Make America Great Again." To Winston, it all feels eerily Orwellian and segregated, like a page ripped from a dystopian novel. He knows that these posters are more than just a display of political support; they are symbols of division and discord.

Winston slows his car and parks it at the side of the road. He watches as the group continues their mission of affixing posters. The atmosphere causes visible tension as pedestrians pass by, some supporting their efforts while others shake their heads in disapproval. Winston knows that America is on the verge of going down a rabbit hole that would swallow it whole. Right then and there, he decides to scrap the article he is writing about "Eco-lining, the New Green Gentrification of America" and begins working on an article that he believes the entire world needs to read.

Winston watches the exchanges between passersby and the members of the group putting up the posters. He watches until the seeds of the article he knows he needs to write begin to sprout. He gets back in his car, narrowly missing getting hit by the cars zooming by much too fast in the area near downtown. He barely notices; his mind is already at his destination, his hands drumming the steering wheel as if he were already typing.

He takes the long route driving to the office, just to allow for more time for his idea to germinate. He is still lost in thought, not even remembering how he got to his desk. But suddenly, he is.

Winston relaxes in his well-worn office chair, reminiscing about the astonishingly peculiar tales he was told during his childhood at his grandparents' legendary Friday night gatherings. Pumped full of whiskey and Al Green, his grandfather would recount stories of his family's attempt to go North to escape the egregiously racist protocols of the South.

Though just a young boy at the time, those stories left an indelible mark on Winston's mind, igniting the flames of his journalistic potential. But now, as a grown man of thirty-five years old, those accounts settled differently within him. The innocence and naiveté of his youth had given way to a deeper understanding of the complexities of the world. He realized that the stories he had once seen as black and white were often shaded with gray.

At a towering six-foot, two-inches tall, with ebony skin and a short kinky afro, Winston has a better perspective on those colorful stories, knowing that his Blackness is going to be a threat to the majority. As he sits by his desk, his eyes catch the sight of a freshly hung poster from the Atlanta Global News Magazine. The poster glares with a garish display of red, white, and blue and bears the slogan "Make America Great Again." Those four seemingly innocent words hold the weight of an atomic bomb, and for a Black child from the South, he winces at what he knows that it really implies.

Looking back to his keyboard, he begins to feverishly click away at the keys. The moon aptly hangs itself in the night sky as he punctuates the last sentence of his article. He neatly packs his laptop in his bag and heads for the door. On his way out, he pauses at the offending poster that seems to mock him from afar. He deviously scans the empty office and yanks the poster loose. He watches as it softly floats into an awaiting garbage can below. Winston smiles at the discarded advertisement as he leaves the suite.

The next day, Winston's fiancée stands before the mirror, brushing her long black hair that cascades down, framing her creamy tan skin and almond-shaped dark eyes. Lori pauses for a moment, lost in her own reflection, before abruptly waking Winston from his deep sleep with an urgent question, "Are you going to work today?"

Winston begins to mutter, "I…I…"

Lori interrupts, "It's no use pondering that now; wake up! I'm going to be late!"

Winston, still in a daze, slowly opening one eye, inquired, "Late for what exactly?"

"Have you completely forgotten? Today is my graduation rehearsal. Soon, you'll have to refer to me as Dr. Lori Yang!"

Winston gathers himself, throwing back the covers as he fully wakes up. He scoots to the edge of the bed and smiles, saying, "It doesn't have the same ring as Mrs. Lori Gale, but it'll do. Speaking of that, do you really need a degree to administer psychology to children? I mean, they are kinda easy to figure out."

Winston chuckles as he makes his way to the bathroom.

"Ha, ha, funny!" Lori scoffs. "By the way, you never said if you were going to work."

Winston yells from the bathroom, "Yes, I have a new article going live today. I'll drop you off on the way to the office."

"Guess it's a big day for both of us," Lori says. "On that note, I'll be in the car."

As she walks away, she loudly says, "Chop-Chop!"

Lori leaves the room, shutting the door behind her.

Winston shouts, "One day you're gonna be forced to drive the car yourself!"

When Winston arrives at the Atlanta Global News Magazine building, he notices that the office is decorated with several new faces. Most people just ignore him as he passes by, but it's the few who don't that worry him.

As he passes, each one of these new faces looks up, as if they're embedding his image in their brains. They quickly scan him up and down, then stare as he makes his way. He decides to meet their rudeness with kindness.

Winston waves at the new, dour white faces. Their thickening presence is sobering and speaks more than any cordial words they could muster. He smirks at the militant, cartoonish images in his head as he whispers, "Halt, don't go there!"

"Winston…Winston!"

He hears his boss, Mr. DeFazio, the editor of the magazine, beckoning him over through the sea of people milling about.

From the sound of it, it's not the first time his name had been called. So Winston hurries over to greet his boss.

"Good morning, sir," Winston jingles as he enters DeFazio's office that is paned with glass. Anyone could see what went on in the office if they bothered to care enough. Winston felt like he was in a fishbowl every time he went in there, but he kept on his happy face.

"Good morning, my boy. Come on in and have a seat."

DeFazio hurries around the desk to sit down.

DeFazio is a short, balding, and portly White man whose shoes squeak when he walks. It takes everything out of Winston not to giggle whenever DeFazio strolls past him.

As soon as he settles in, DeFazio belts out, "How do you like the new changes?" Before Winston can answer, he goes on. "The Sun is making some improvements. The stories we write will be more ah… conservative."

Winston jumps in before his boss can say more.

"It's funny that you should mention that, I have a new exposé regarding the upcoming election. I think you're going to like it!"

DeFazio replies, "I always do! However, after this one, we're taking our story cues from Fox News. You understand."

Winston shifts in his seat. "I see. In that case, do you want to review the article before it goes live?"

The phone on DeFazio's desk begins to ring.

He rushes Winston off, saying, "No…I trust your judgment. Go ahead and make it live. Be sure to hit the global button too."

With an awkward smile, Winston quietly walks out while DeFazio takes his call.

Winston sits at his desk. He puts his phone on silent and opens his article for one last review. He begins to softly read excepts to himself.

"White America has a desperate need for omnipresence. So much so that it goes out of its way to impress that a savior is on his way to reset a historically repugnant clock."

His eyes dance as he goes on.

"The Make America Great Again slogan is nothing more than a weakly masked codex for a great many sentiments. It resonates loud and clear that People of Color have to go back into the decrepit bottle of slavery. Or at the very least, Blacks should be put back under the control of the White gaze. It is the effective dog whistle being used by this Presidential candidate and unfortunately, it is associated with his campaign's negatively suggested policies and weaponizing rhetoric.

While some people view the MAGA slogan as a call for patriotism and national pride, those that are of color do not! There are several reasons why it is widely regarded as bad and problematic. Its Orwellian views are a recipe for disaster and pull at the already fragile threads of a teetering American society."

After reviewing, Winston uploads it onto the AGNM's server. Concentrating on the screen, he mumbles the various release options. Muttering, "Internal, External, Electronic Media, and Global Release."

He takes a deep breath as he depresses each button on the cumbersome content management system. His direct editor never had time to read his work and probably wouldn't have understood it anyway. And copy editors had been let go long ago. So Winston had painstakingly gone through his column to avoid any typos or grammatical errors. He didn't want small mistakes to muddle his big message. He gives the column one last read. Satisfied, he nods his head and looks around.

He takes another deep breath and mutters, "Here we go."

Finally, he clicks one last green button that says "Go Live." Then he slowly pushes the enter key. The column titled "Make America Great Again…The Battle Cry of Sleeper Racists" is live. He nervously exhales, closes his laptop, and walks out of the office for an appointment.

As Winston cruises down the street, his mobile phone incessantly pings, demanding his attention. The deluge of notifications is so overwhelming that he has no choice but to veer off into a nearby grocery store parking lot to review his notifications. They're all from his email, so he opens the app.

However, he isn't prepared for what he sees. His work email box overflows with an avalanche of messages from what appears to be a multitude of reporters, numerous news outlets, and even Mr. DeFazio himself. Upon closer review, Winston grins at the beautifully worded messages of gratitude and support from people all over the United States.

Unfortunately, this was short-lived. The remaining messages that overflowed his inbox were of pure visceral disdain. He took a moment to look at the odd juxtaposition laid out for him in daunting detail.

Winston realizes that his inbox was a literal microcosm of a fractured America, right there in black and white. The sentiments were polarizing, to say the least. One message, in particular, from an unknown sender commanded his attention. It said, "There is nowhere to hide. Wherever you go, WE will find you!"

Sweat streams down his forehead as he lays his phone down on the passenger seat, desperately trying to escape the relentless notifications. Winston's mind races with a mixture of anxiety and apprehension, unsure of how to handle the flood of messages that await his attention.

He continues to sit there, feeling paralyzed by the weight of the situation, his mind torn between confronting the emails or fleeing from them altogether. The car's interior seems to close in on him, a suffocating cocoon of indecision, as he grapples with the choice that could unravel the already fragile threads of his life.

Winston knows that there is nowhere to hide. Shutting his eyes, he attempts to calm his racing thoughts, but even in the darkness, he can't escape the vision of himself stepping into the office the next day. The imagined scenario plays out like a well-executed scene from a horror movie. The office door creaks open slowly as if moved by unseen hands, and he steps inside, the cold, sterile atmosphere closing in around him like a vice.

The hum of the fluorescent lights above seems to grow louder, casting eerie shadows across the empty desks. As he walks further into the office, the sense of foreboding deepens, and he can almost hear the whispers of his coworkers, their faces contorted into grotesque masks of disapproval.

His colleagues angrily gather like a lynch mob with DeFazio at the helm, holding the rope. Winston shakes himself out of his anxiety and his imagined reception dissipates. Winston starts the car, but his demeanor seems devoid of any emotion resembling that of a soulless automaton.

He drives home with an almost mechanical precision, his thoughts distant and detached from the reality around him. The streets blur by, their vibrant colors reduced to a dull, monochrome backdrop as the weight of his predicament presses upon him like a leaden shroud.

Sunlight blazes through the windows of Winston's bedroom, illuminating the dust particles suspended in the air like fleeting memories. He rolls over to see Lori still sleeping, her peaceful state a stark contrast to the turmoil that churns within him. He dares not wake her, thinking, "It's for the best. She doesn't need to see me in this condition."

He moves quietly throughout their apartment as he showers and dresses to drive to the office. Winston knows that if his email inbox is overflowing, that DeFazio's will be too. And their fears, like their political leanings, probably won't align. It leaves him more than uneasy.

With every thought of his impending meeting with DeFazio, Winston's stomach somersaults, and a pervasive sense of unease settles over him like a dark cloud, casting a long shadow over the morning light.

The mere prospect of facing DeFazio fills him with a mix of anxiety and trepidation. This isn't the first time one of his columns has caused a stir, but this time feels different. Winston isn't sure if he has committed career suicide or thrown the country a lifeline—either way, he doesn't feel good about it.

He takes one last pause at the mirror before walking out the door, the reflection staring back at him shows a mask of uncertainty and determination. He reassures himself in a hushed murmur, "It is what it is... it had to be done."

As he closes the door behind him, he carries the weight of his choices and the consequences that await, the echoes of his self-doubt fading into the distance with each determined step.

Arriving at the office, he steps through the heavy wooden doors of the building and into the cool shadows of the interior, a shiver coursing down his spine as he senses a strange, palpable energy in the air. He hurries through the lobby and boards the elevator. As he ascends, the imaginary smell of death and decay seems to waft through the confined space.

Then, with a dissonant chime, the elevator doors slide open on his floor. With a deep breath, he pushes through the waiting people whose faces are etched with cluelessness about his outward anxiety. He steps onto the 14th floor, casting a long shadow across the threshold of his place of work.

Once he enters the office, the silence is absolute. He stands in the doorway, taking a few moments to settle his thoughts. That's when he sees it. The entire office seems to galvanize into one angry entity. Despite having imagined it countless times in the last twenty-four hours, nothing could have truly prepared him for witnessing it in living color. He's never seen anything like it, and he's terrified!

The tension hangs in the air like thick, cold honey, palpable and suffocating. Their eyes bore an intense, quiet rage that sends a shiver down Winston's spine, causing the hairs on his neck to stand at attention.

DeFazio emerges after walking through the crowd and shatters the oppressive silence with a venomous command.

"Winston Gale…My office... NOW!"

He turns abruptly and strides toward his office, leaving Winston no choice but to take a deep breath and obediently follow the path that DeFazio has carved through the sea of his co-workers' furious faces. The atmosphere is charged with tension and hostility, making each step feel like he's entering the "Door of No Return."

Upon reaching the office, Winston's phone buzzes insistently. He glances quickly down and sees that it's an incoming call from Lori. Anxious to focus on the impending confrontation with DeFazio, he promptly sends the call to voicemail. As he stands in the doorway, he can't help but notice a fuming DeFazio, hunched over his desk, emanating an aura of seething frustration.

DeFazio explodes, his voice sharp and furious, "What the fuck were you thinking? You labeled the man and his entire campaign as racist... to the entire world, no less!"

With his finger raised in the air, Winston attempts to explain, "Sir, I understand this is a sensitive and polarizing topic, but if you'd just take a moment to consider the facts presented in the article, you will see—"

DeFazio's red-faced rage silences Winston, his words swallowed by DeFazio's cold stare, leaving them both trapped in the eye of a professional storm.

DeFazio rudely interrupts him, "I don't give a damn about the facts! Politics isn't about facts; it's about winning. The Atlanta Global News Magazine has aligned itself with winners. You're making America look like that one weird kid at the park kicking squirrels, for God's sake!"

His voice boomed with frustration and disappointment, leaving Winston momentarily taken aback by his boss's reaction. The weight of DeFazio's words settled heavily on his shoulders, like an anchor dragging him even further.

Winston squirmed uncomfortably in his seat as DeFazio relentlessly tore into his "ill-timed" article. The tongue-lashing showed no signs of ending, so Winston was forced to mitigate the attack.

"Sir," he interrupted, his voice edged with determination, "I apologize if the timing of the article is inconvenient, but it remains not only relevant but undeniably true." His words hung in the air like a gauntlet thrown. Winston steeled himself for the repercussions of his unwavering commitment to the truth.

DeFazio's face flushed with anger, and he rose from his chair, his voice dripping with sarcasm.

"Well, here's a proposition for you, Winston. You can either swallow your pride and retract that article or, if you prefer, indulge your literary talents in a sea of fluff pieces. The choice is all yours but in the meantime…Get the Hell out of my office!"

Winston defiantly stormed out of DeFazio's office and returned to his desk. He pulled out his phone, dialed the number of his best friend, Mike, and pressed it against his ear with a sense of frustration.

"Hey, Mike," he said with an apologetic tone, "I'm sorry to call you during work hours, but if you have a moment, could you give me a callback? I really need to talk." After ending the call, Winston gathered his belongings and left the office.

CHAPTER TWO

That night, Winston is drawn into a dream where he plays the lead role in a modern-day black-and-white film. He's wearing a letterman's jacket with the name "Freddy" embroidered on the front. As he moves through the moonlit open field, an eerie glow casts in the distance, revealing an abandoned farmhouse down the way. A sense of terror grips him as he sprints desperately for shelter. Upon reaching the porch, he comes to a sudden halt, his eyes fixating on the street number: "433."

The movie is being watched by a sea of White people in a darkened theater; many of them are wearing white hoodies that are draped low over their faces. Ominous music plays while Freddy quietly enters the home. Moonlight filters through and the sparse light showcases the tattered curtains, casting ethereal beams that illuminate a dirty and worn interior. The soft glow reveals the state of disrepair of the old home. He panics as the creaking floorboards seem to echo his movement throughout the hopefully empty house.

As Freddy stumbles around in the farmhouse, he accidentally stubs his foot. Something skitters across the floor, catching his attention. He looks down and, within the black and white film, an empty dog bowl appears in a shade of green. Across the front of the bowl, the name "Cheetah" is prominently displayed.

Curtains wave gently, even without a breeze. Freddy flinches as eerie shadows loom on the walls, causing him to shrink fearfully. The ominous sound of footsteps and whispers echoes in the darkness, prompting Freddy to back away in one direction, then another. Each creak or sudden movement sends shivers down his spine.

Meanwhile, in the audience, laughter and jeers erupted loudly. Various audience members mock him, screeching, "You're an idiot! Just leave! No one is there! Dude, what are you scared of? They're always the first to die!"

The laughter continues, mingled with indistinct chatter. Freddy's terror intensifies as he remains trapped within the horror movie, and then, abruptly, he's pulled from it and thrust back into Winston's sleeping body, jolting him awake.

Winston's body is drenched in cold sweat as he abruptly sits up in bed. With a trembling hand, he wipes the perspiration from his forehead. He takes a careful glance toward Lori, hoping that he did not wake her. His chest heaves as he fights to catch his breath. In the dim light, he checks the time on the clock before slithering out of bed. The tiny panels on the digital clock flip to 4:33 a.m. He rolls out of bed and walks toward the bathroom.

Still covered in sweat, Winston stands motionless before the mirror, his gaze riveted upon his reflection. Winston can't shake the nightmare, leaving him with an uncanny sensation that Freddy's presence lingers in the image staring back at him. He turns on the cold water and splashes his face, the cool water offering some relief.

He then grabs a hand towel, gently patting himself dry. Afterward, he opens the medicine cabinet and retrieves a pill bottle with his name on it, labeled "ZENCITRAVMASI 500mg." Two round, inky-black pills spill into the palm of his hand. Winston hesitates for a moment, his eyes locked on the pills. Then, with a decisive yet almost automatic movement, he swallows them down.

Later that morning, the tiny kitchenette in Winston and Lori's cozy apartment echoes with the clinking of dishes and the subtle fragrance of bread toasting in the oven. Lori, with her tousled hair and a hint of sleep still lingering in her eyes, makes her way over to the radio perched on the laminated countertop. With a playful grin, she clicks it on.

Lori muses, "Let's find out what's going on in Hotlanta today. Not having cable is just about to take its toll."

The radio comes to life, filling the room with the lively tunes of a local station. Lori can't help but dance a little as she moves about the kitchen, reaching for ingredients and a saucer.

But Winston, sitting at the small kitchen table with his eyes fixed somewhere between the tabletop and his thoughts, doesn't seem to respond to her comment.

Lori pauses for a moment, glancing over at him. His usually bright eyes are clouded with a somber mood, a heaviness that seems to hang over him like a shroud. She worries and sets her breakfast aside.

She softly asks, "Hey… You okay?" As she speaks, the radio abruptly stops playing the cheerful melody that had filled the room.

A commercial bursts through the speakers, its words echoing with an uncanny resonance.

"If you're having frequent feelings of uncontrollable anger, fear, paranoia, defiance to authority, disorientation, or recurring dizziness, you're not alone. ZENCITRAVMASI has helped countless sufferers get their lives under control. If you have Medicaid or Medicare, you could qualify for 25% off of your ZENCITRAVMASI prescription. Contact your physician now for details."

Winston's gaze drifts to the radio, his brow furrowing at the eerily fitting description. Lori exchanges a concerned glance with him, their shared thoughts unspoken but hanging heavily in the air. The commercial ends and the music comes back on. Winston shakes it off with a visible shake of his head and pours a cup of coffee, then sits back down at the small kitchen table.

Grabbing his tablet, he taps his finger on the notifications which indicate that he has several messages. His eyes lock in on a familiar conversation thread with Mike. Their conversation seems to carry an unspoken weight that leaves him momentarily lost in thought.

Winston reads the exchange to himself. Winston had asked, "Did I make the right decision?"

Mike's response, quick and to the point, was enough to bring him back to the present. He couldn't help but read the message several times, contemplating its significance. Mike wrote, "Bro, are you in love with Lori, or in obligation? Hit me back when you can and let's talk about that, and about whatever happened the other day. Ttyl."

Winston's heart sinks slightly as he digests Mike's words. It is a question he has asked himself more than once, especially lately. His relationship with Lori has been a journey of highs and lows, and it's true that they have faced their fair share of challenges. He has always cared deeply for her, but is it love or just a sense of duty that's keeping them together?

A stern look comes over Winston's face. He exits his text messages and re-opens his work emails. Meanwhile, Lori continues her morning routine, her movements a touch more serene as she butters her toast and takes a seat at the small kitchen table. Breakfast is turning out to be a quiet affair, with the radio playing softly in the background.

She glances at him with concern and asks, "Another rough one, huh?"

Winston continues to read, and without looking up, he replies with a question of his own, "Meaning?"

Lori nibbles on her toast across from him.

Lori can't hold back any longer, her concern evident as she responds, "Well, since you're going to make me say it. You had another bad dream. That makes three in as many weeks."

She takes a big bite out of her toast, trying to break the tension.

Winston looks up with a wry smile and a hint of playfulness in his voice, "Psychoanalyzing me again, I see."

Lori can't help but smile and replies, "I sure am. That child psychology Degree is finally paying off!"

Winston grins in response.

"Together three years now, and your sarcasm is still sexy as ever!"

Their laughter fills the small kitchen as Lori playfully flicks toast crumbs in his direction. Winston smiles, shaking his head, and dusts the crumbs off his shirt and tablet, their easy banter momentarily dispelling the earlier somber mood.

"Seriously, you ought to be enjoying sweet dreams, not having nightmares," Lori insists. She reaches over and lovingly takes his hand in hers. "You're doing so well, and Atlanta Global is getting major attention thanks to you! My man happens to be their only award-winning columnist—"

Winston interjects, “Slash journalist!”

Lori continues, “Exactly, which is precisely why you’re in the running for a promotion. So, tell me, what’s really bothering you?”

Winston lets out a sigh.

“I don’t know. There are lots of changes going on at the office. A lot of new faces and none of them seem to be getting any darker, if you know what I mean. And that MAGA article did not help the situation.”

Lori tries to console him, sounding almost as weary as he looked.

“Babe, it’s one questionable article out of the hundreds of great articles you’ve written. Get out of your head and focus on the good stuff. A promotion will put us in the position to get that house we’ve been looking at. Not to mention all those babies you keep talking about. Believe me, this article thing will blow over in a couple of weeks. Life is good!”

Lori smiles, and Winston nods in agreement as he packs his work bag. He shoots Lori a half-hearted smile and stands up from the table.

Lori shifts gears, asking, “Are we eating out tonight?”

Winston replies, “Sure, I kinda have a taste for Chinese.”

Lori smiles seductively and prances over to Winston, saying, “Well, you can eat in for that.”

Laughing, Winston says, “I’ll see you tonight.”

He kisses Lori on the forehead and leaves.

As Winston strolls through the park near his workplace, he reflects on Lori’s advice with a smile. He gazes up at the bright blue sky, sips his coffee, and casts aside his feelings of doom and gloom. Upon reaching his office building, he looks up at the marquee which reads “Lux Towers” and smiles once more before entering.

Although the building is under renovation, The lobby is abuzz with activity, and there's a mix of pastries and coffee wafting through the air. People chatter as they walk by, while others attempt to devour their breakfast as quickly as possible.

Winston casually walks through the lobby making pleasant morning gestures to the security guards and others. As he arrives at the elevator, the doors open up and he jovially steps in.

When Winston reaches his floor, he is surprised to see several maintenance workers outside his office suite, changing the sign on the door. One of them is painting over a mural of a diverse group of people having fun in the park with blinding white paint. The sign that's coming down reads, "Atlanta Global Media." The new name that is going up says, "The Southern Republic."

Upon entering the office, Winston observes a construction crew disassembling the old cubicles that had housed a predominantly African-American staff of reporters on one side. As he surveys the expansive space, he notices that new cubicles are being installed on the other side. To his surprise, several young White males in white hoodies and trendy jeans have already taken occupancy there.

Shaking his head in disbelief, he goes straight to his still-standing old cubicle, placing his bag down. From an adjacent partition emerges a brown-skinned man with a beard; it is Lilbert Lewis, Winston's coworker and close friend. Lilbert is the resident geek of the office and has a deep love for all things Anime.

Lilbert's cubicle is adorned with toy bobbleheads featuring his favorite characters. Lilbert isn't being trendy with his beard; he has a unique stance on shaving, claiming it provides natural protection against sun-induced skin cancer.

He and Winston often engage in spirited debates on this topic. Lilbert nods at Winston with concern as they both observe the guys in hoodies laughing and chatting nearby.

Winston cautions, “Two months ago, they said we were in a hiring freeze. Guess they didn’t get the memo.”

Lilbert scoffs, “Look at ‘em ... jeans, hoodies. When I started here, we…,” and continues with a lowered voice as he looks around, then points to the skin on the back of his hand, “Couldn’t walk in without wearing a jacket and tie.”

Winston glances at the back of Lilbert’s hand and notices tiny white spots, quickly averting his eyes.

Winston responds, “It seems times are changing.”

Lilbert frowns. “Yeah, I guess so.”

Then, he immediately brightens up, saying, “But you don’t have anything to worry about. You’re the best columnist here, and I hear you’re a lock for the investigative journalist promotion. Hell, you’ll probably be running this place one day.”

Winston grins, shaking his head in disbelief as he scoots in front of his computer, and says, “Yeah, well, I’m already doing the work, but we’ll see.”

Later that evening, Winston and Lori cozy up on the couch, engrossed in a television program. Lori redirects her attention to Winston, her face breaking into a warm smile. Lori observes, “You’re in a good mood.”

Winston replies, “I’ve been reflecting on what you said, and you know what? We’ve got a lot going for us. Life IS good!”

Lori smiles contentedly and quips, “See! I’m glad you’ve come around to my way of thinking.”

As Winston tenderly kisses her forehead, they both settle back in to enjoy the show. Yet, beneath his outward demeanor, Winston can’t shake a nagging sense of unease.

The following day, Winston enters the freshly rebranded “Southern Republic” office cautiously. The atmosphere is charged with tension. The cubicles that were once a hub of diversity now stand nearly deserted.

He proceeds past the all-White male security officers. As he walks by, one of the officers scowls and places his hand on his holstered weapon. With every step he takes, Winston feels a mounting sense of panic, the onset of a potential panic attack becoming increasingly imminent.

The next day, Winston arrives at his cubicle to find that Lilbert is gone. This was unusual because he generally was the first to arrive and the last to leave. Lilbert's workspace was completely empty. It was devoid of Lilbert's files, computer, and all of his signature knick-knacks. Winston quickly stood up from his chair and scanned the office, thinking Lilbert's desk was relocated during the restructuring. Winston glossed over the cubicles in other departments, but still…nothing.

While Winston was mulling the ever-changing landscape of the new "Southern Republic," a fellow colleague smugly paraded by, her pace slowing to a crawl as she took the time to shoot Winston a scowl.

Winston huffs and shouts in her direction, "Well, it's good to see you too, Cassie!"

Suddenly, She stops, turns around toward Winston, and rubs her neck in an oddly threatening manner. She sharply replies, "Times are changing around here, for the better...for "US."

Winston waves her off and replies, "Whatever, "CRASSIE!" She gave a sly smile before she sauntered away, leaving Winston speechless about the strange turn of events.

Winston decides to give Lilbert a call. After ringing several times, the voicemail outgoing message plays.

He whispers, "Hey buddy…where did they move you to? Not used to seeing an empty chair. Hit me back."

A calendar alert pings from Winston's computer, alerting him of a deadline for a piece that he is working on. He refocuses and dives into the article.

Time seems to slip away, and before he realizes it, the workday is drawing to a close. Curious if Lilbert has responded, Winston powers on his phone, but no messages have arrived. With a sigh, he packs up his belongings and heads out for the evening.

The next morning, Winston arrives at work as usual. He wanders over to his desk and sits down. He unzips his work bag and retrieves the files he had taken home the previous night. As he mindlessly opens his desk drawer, his eyes widen, and the color drains from his face.

There, inside the drawer, rests a noose in the tray. In shock, Winston drops his files and leaps to his feet, screaming, "What the fuck!"

There was no response. It was as if no one had heard him, or was even paying him any attention.

He quickly stands, furrowing his brow as he scrutinizes everyone in the office. Several of his White co-workers stare back at him, seemingly nonchalant. A security guard appears in his peripheral view, whispering into a walkie-talkie before heading in Winston's direction.

Gripping the noose, Winston pushes past the guard and hurries to his manager's office.

Winston looks through the smudged glass door and sees Mr. DeFazio, behind his desk, reading over documents. Winston plants himself in the doorway, visibly shaken. He looks up and smiles at Winston, chirping, "Come on in. Whatcha' got there?"

Winston begins shaking the noose in the air. He angrily shouts, "It's a fuckin' noose! It was in my desk drawer. Somebody here is threatening my life."

Winston turns to peer out of DeFazio's glass-paneled office wall. He grimaces at the sea of cubicles in the writer's bullpen, sickened that they're almost all now occupied by nothing but White people.

Winston mumbles, "Hell...probably everybody!" He looks back at DeFazio as he leans back in his chair unfazed.

"Threat?...no." DeFazio is almost casual in his dismissal. "They're just having a bit of fun. Hell, I found a dead mouse in my bag last week. You're taking things too seriously."

Winston fumed.

"A dead mouse ain't a noose. In the four years that I've been working here, I've never gotten a noose in my drawer. This is because of that article I wrote. Actually, this stunt proves my point! Make America Great Again means no Blacks allowed!"

Suddenly, DeFazio flips a MAGA hat onto his desk, remarking, "This is my MAGA...zine. I don't like your tone, and I don't feel safe with you around here. Maybe you'll be more comfortable at BET!"

Furious, Winston scoffs, "BET?"

DeFazio pops his cap on his head, crossing his arms, yelling, "Clean out your desk and take your Nigger Necktie with you!"

Winston seems to swell as he looms over DeFazio, asking, "What the hell did you just say to me?"

DeFazio boldly stares at Winston, pressing the intercom on his desk phone. He makes an announcement to the entire office while deadpanning, declaring to the entire office, "Winston Gale has been terminated!"

Then he swiftly takes his finger off the button with an enormous grin on his face.

Winston turns around to see all those alabaster, cold faces staring back at him.

He screams, “You know what...Fuck you muthafuckas!”

Winston storms out, marches to his cubicle, and grabs his bag to leave the office. Before he can make it to the door, he notices a janitor removing his photos and plaques from the wall and tossing them into a waste basket. Winston hesitates for a moment, then snatches the last award from the janitor’s hand and leaves.

As he exits the building, his cell phone rings. He pauses for a moment to read the screen; it says “Chicago Blaze Publication.”

Winston answers, “Hello?”

The caller asks, “Is this Winston Gale, the columnist and journalist?”

Winston sighs to himself and says, “Yes, it is. Who’s calling?”

The caller replies, “My name is Marguerite Turner, and I’m the CEO of The Chicago Blaze Publication. We are a premier online publication for African-American global news.”

Winston excitedly said, “Yes, of course. I know all about your publication!”

Marguerite goes on, “I don’t typically make these calls myself, but the article you wrote about MAGA impressed us a lot! What do you think about coming on board with our organization in Chicago?”

Winston drops his boxes and remains hushed, surprised at the timing of the call.

She asks, “Mr. Gale... Are you there?”

No longer certain what to think, he replies, “I’m sorry... Yes. I’m here. Can I get back to you on that?”

She comments, “Yes, of course. I would not expect an answer on our very first phone call. However, time waits for no man. I will need an answer within the next 48 hours. Talk to you then.”

She ends the call.

CHAPTER THREE

That night, Winston arrives home, his career packed in a cardboard box. Lori sits in the living room, drinking a glass of red wine and engrossed in the news. Upon his entrance, she maintains her focus on the TV as the anchor announces a popular railroad company's expansion into the Atlanta area.

With a sigh, she quips, "Babe, it looks like Atlanta's future is all about train tracks, apartment complexes, and Waffle Houses... Geez!"

Winston heaves a deep sigh, his fingertips tracing a melancholic melody on the box he clutches.

Lori instantly glances up, noticing Winston's unusual demeanor. She gasps, letting out a startled squeal that causes her to spill wine on the table.

She blurts out, "Winston, why are you holding that box? What's happening?"

Winston sets the box down and spends the better part of the evening sharing the details of what happened.

Later that evening, after Lori has gone to bed, Winston grapples with the events and challenges surrounding his tenure at the magazine.

His phone suddenly rings, and he hurriedly answers, saying, "Hello."

On the other end, he recognizes the familiar voice of his friend, Mike, who apologizes for calling so late due to a hectic day.

Winston mutes the television and speaks quietly, replying, "I understand. Seems like 'crazy' is the theme lately."

Mike replies, "I'm all ears. Talk to me."

Winston's voice drops, carrying a mix of frustration and disappointment. "Mike, I need to tell you the whole story. I was fired, and it wasn't just a regular firing. My boss suddenly decided that he's a racist. I confronted him about finding a noose in my desk drawer and it all went downhill from there."

Mike exclaims, "A noose?!" His anger flares at the revelation. "That's some bullshit! You absolutely did the right thing by confronting him about that."

Winston continues, "Yeah, but it cost me my job. The whole conservative rebranding situation was toxic, and I couldn't stay there any longer."

Mike's tone turns empathetic. "I get it, Win. Sometimes walking away is the only way to keep your dignity intact. Now, about that job offer in Chicago, you should seriously consider it. You deserve a fresh start in a better environment."

Winston nods in agreement, saying, "I'm really leaning that way, Mike. It feels like a new chapter, and I need that right now."

Concerned for Winston, Mike inquires, "And what's your take on the Lori situation? Are you planning to work things out?"

Winston leans back, contemplating his response. "I've been giving it a lot of thought. I do love her, no doubt about that. It's just that I've been experiencing some culture shock."

Mike chuckles and teases, "You've been together for years, and you're still adjusting to being with a Chinese woman?"

Winston replies with a playful laugh, saying, "I see you've got jokes!"

Their conversation continues, delving into the complexities of Winston's situation, his future plans, and more about the opportunities in Chicago. They chat late into the night.

Several weeks later, Winston and Lori diligently pack boxes and bags with their cherished belongings. The room is adorned with plastic-wrapped furniture, including a piano with sheet music scattered on top.

The walls bear witness to their family history, displaying several framed photos. One captures the loving image of Winston's mother, another showcases his great-grandparents, and yet another photo includes Winston's mother, grandmother, and sister.

He methodically removes books from the shelf, carefully inspecting each one as he goes. In his hands, he holds three distinct volumes, their covers and spines Prominently displayed. Among the selections are "Outwitting The Devil" by Napoleon Hill, "The Great Migration in Historical Perspective" by Joe William-Trotter, and "Melanin: The Chemical Key To Black Greatness" by Carol Barnes. Lori walks over and peers over Winston's shoulder, concern etched on her face.

"I understand the need to leave Atlanta, I really do. But why Chicago? It feels like we're trading hot peaches for cold bullets."

Winston shrugs with a reply, "The Chicago Blaze Publication is offering me a fantastic opportunity. It comes with a better salary, and I'll be able to write stories that truly make a difference."

He gently takes her hands in his and continues. “I know this is a major move for both of us, but we don’t have much of a choice. I’m not proud of it…but I’ve kept something from you. After I published that article, we started receiving death threats.”

Winston continues, “And when I found that box on our doorstep, it really put things into perspective. Moving away from here is the only way I can protect you.”

Lori looks baffled, asking, “Wait, what box? What was in the box?”

Winston sighs, “Just some shit! I didn’t want to worry you.”

Winston reflected on the day he opened his front door. On the doorstep lay a boot-sized shoebox. He glanced around, scanning the street in all directions, before cautiously leaning down to open the box. As he lifted the lid, he revealed two burlap dolls resting inside—one black and the other yellow, both adorned with nooses around their necks.

Lori brushes off Winston’s comments with a scoff, “All this fuss over some dolls?” She continues packing, remarking, “Yeah, I’m not worried. I don’t need your protection for that.”

Nervously, Winston insists, “Yes, you do! When Trump announced his candidacy, everything changed with that ‘Make America Great Again’ slogan. Now the good ol’ boy brigade has taken over the office, and I’m fired. Chicago is the first real opportunity I’ve had since then. That’s why we gotta move.”

Lori stands speechless. Then asks, “How did I get wrapped up in this?”

Winston thinks Lori should know more. She would want to move out of Atlanta as much as he did if she knew the terrible truth about what she thought were just hollow threats. Lori doesn’t know that she has been directly threatened. No, make that targeted.

Winston replies, "They know you're with me. One of those individuals mentioned you by name. He even knows where and when you get off the train every day. We both need to leave!"

Lori stares blankly, her hand inching towards her neck as fear overtakes her expression. "They're watching me?"

Winston nods slowly, confirming, "Yes."

Winston reassures her, saying, "We're going to be okay. I have a plan. Chicago is our best option. Besides, all signs point North! It's been a recurring theme for Black people, especially in my family."

"Well, Chicago isn't exactly North. It's the Midwest," Lori responds with a half-hearted smile as she clears her throat. "Anyway, look at all the Black people leaving Chicago to come to Atlanta."

Winston pushes back, "Technically, that's not true."

Lori playfully bounces from side to side. Lori begins to pace in a straight line, using her fingers to count. "Let's start with the rappers. Exhibit 'A,' Ludacris, Common, and even Kanye, at one point in time."

Winston zips, "First of all, it's 'Yeezy,' and he was actually born in Atlanta and then moved to Chicago where he became infamously insane. And speaking of Kanye...he has a whole-ass baby that's literally named 'North.'"

They both laugh as Lori returns to packing.

Winston continues, "It's not just about Black people. Just look at your Asian family. They found the land of 'Milk and Money' right here in umm...NORTH America."

With a sense of comical accomplishment, Winston gracefully bows and exclaims, "Thank you very much!"

Lori chuckles and playfully tosses a towel at Winston while giggling.

Winston adds, “Hell, you High-Key Republican anyway. Yet you live on the Democratic side of town like you’re really down. You ain’t never seen a Trumper campaigning at Greenbriar Mall.” Lori dismissively waves Winston off.

Winston says, “Yeah... that’s what I thought.”

Lori sets aside her packing and approaches him, gently rubbing his arm.

“Seriously, babe, why didn’t you tell me all this before? I just turned down a job in Tennessee. Chicago is so far away. I mean, I’d follow you anywhere, but it’s gotta make sense.”

Winston nods in agreement, placing his books on the desk before taking a seat.

His demeanor turning serious, “I never told you this, but my great-grandparents were part of the Great Migration. They always spoke about leaving the redneck South for the welcoming White arms of the North. Unfortunately, they left and were never heard from again. I gotta find out what happened to them.”

Suddenly, Lori looks annoyed while Winston looks away. Then her demeanor quickly changes to sympathetic when Winston makes eye contact with her. She puts on a pouty face and says, “This is kinda heavy.”

But then she brightens up, suggesting, “I know what you need, a distraction...how about a blow job?”

Somewhat surprised by her offer. Winston stops what he’s doing and replies, “Oooh…kay?”

Lori smiles and they kiss. The kiss grows more heavy and intimate.

The long-awaited day for their faithful move has finally come. Winston and Lori go from room to room, taking a final look at the place where they have spent the last few years together.

Lori leans affectionately on Winston and says, "It's time to go, let's create new memories."

Winston winces and tightens his grip on his favorite duffel bag.

The pair, heavy with several bags and luggage, walk toward the door. Lori stops short of the door. She puts down her things and runs over to the piano. She grabs a black notebook and puts it in her purse.

She walks back to the door where Winston is.

He greets her with a joke. "Of course, we can't forget your notebook full of music. Hopefully, you'll finish writing that damn song one day. For the life of me...I don't know why you're not a famous concert pianist."

Lori confides, "You know why. Good Chinese daughters study what their parents tell them to. Speaking of books," she asks, "Are you bringing them with us?"

Winston replies, "Nope, not this time."

Lori gasps, responding, "Really?! I've never seen you without one."

Winston assures her, "They'll be waiting for me in Chicago. My sister, Chloe, will make sure of that."

"Oh, that reminds me, let's make a quick stop on the way," Lori suggests. "I need to pick up a puzzle book; you know I love a good riddle to solve."

Winston happily agrees, "Sure thing, let's go."

He scans the room, noticing his desk cluttered with books. In the midst of the pile, he spots a pill bottle.

He drops his bags and rushes to retrieve it, shaking the bottle to hear the pills rattle. Winston exclaims, "Can't forget these!"

The pair leaves and closes the door behind them.

Winston packs the trunk of his black, four-door, 2012 Toyota Camry with their bags. While he does so, Lori quietly nestles herself in the passenger seat and fiddles with the radio. Moments later, the engine roars to life, and they begin their journey down the road.

They listen to music as they drive down a desolate road in the backwoods of Georgia. Winston coyly looks over at Lori, a weird grin plastered on his face, and says, "You are so beautiful! How did I get so lucky to have a woman like you?"

Smirking, Lori cautiously asks, "Oh shit...what have you done now?"

"You know, they say it's easier to seek forgiveness than permission, right?"

Lori's face wears a grim expression as she hastily lowers the music's volume. Her voice cracks as she replies, "Yeah... yeah."

Winston beams, flashing a full-toothed smile, and continues, "I was thinking, we could turn this short trip into a telling experience. Let's make stops at some quirky hotels and off-road B&B spots along the way. What do you say?"

Lori's demeanor changes from relaxed to irked.

She responds with a hint of surliness, "Great! Now this trip is going to feel like it lasts a whole week. I don't think there's much to see in these parts. Whatever's in these butt-fuck woods…it's hidden back here for a reason." She shrugs her shoulders and adds, "But hey, it could be fun!"

Winston periodically glances at Lori with concern as he drives. He begins, "It's not just about having fun, you know. My family kinda made me feel like there were more things other than racist White folks that stopped Black people from getting out. There's something to it when you consider the sheer number of people who went missing. I feel like I owe it to my family to trace the paths they might have taken to head North."

Winston thinks back to when he was a boy, listening to his great aunts and uncles telling stories at family gatherings about the day their sister, Nora, and her husband, Wilbur, left Georgia, heading for Chicago. That day was filled with excitement and concern because the road was never safe for Black people back then.

"Uncle Joe said, 'Nora wasn't scared of nothing! She walked around town in Macon, Georgia, like she owned the place. Them White folks just about left her and Wilbur alone. I think that's what gave them the notion to go North on they own.'"

Winston snaps back to the conversation, saying, "Not to mention, this trip could open even bigger doors for me in investigative journalism,"

Winston muses with enthusiasm. "I can picture it now, me on the cover of TIME magazine, holding my Pulitzer." Winston smiles, waving his hand in the air as if showcasing the headlines. "'The Hate Migration... Will it ever end?'"

Lori brushes it off, saying, "I get it, babe, but it's 2015. White and Black people have been good for a long time. I mean, just look at us fulfilling interracial couple goals!"

Winston side-eyes Lori in a gesture of friendly disagreement.

As they drive down the road, a billboard with an arrow for a hotel in a hick town called Jekyll Falls, Georgia, looms on the roadside. They decide to take the exit. After navigating a dimly lit and winding road, the couple finds themselves in the eerie and deteriorating parking lot of the Jekyll Inn & Breakfast.

The dated hotel is nestled deep in the backwoods, close to old railroad tracks. The inn bears a design reminiscent of an aging

Holiday Inn, featuring rusted wrought iron accents and a murky pool. Loose gravel popcorns through the air, creating a crackling sound under their tires as they slow down near the entrance.

Winston circles around and parks near the center of the lot before opening the door. Lori casts a sideways glance at him and inquires, “Why do you always park in the middle of the lot, especially when it’s empty?”

He shrugs his shoulders and replies, “Everyone rushes to park right in front. They’ll even squeeze into spaces that don’t quite fit just to be closer. I’d rather avoid anyone accidentally hitting my car.”

Lori groans, shaking her head from side to side as she taps on her phone.

Winston steps out of the car, leans in, and adds, “Just watch, this lot will be filled up by morning, and we’ll have no problems getting out of here.”

With that, he gives Lori a smile, closes the door, and makes his way to the hotel. Lori stays behind, browsing through her phone.

Winston reaches the glass entrance doors and hesitates before pulling the handles, taken aback by the grimy doors and windows.

He mutters, “They can’t be serious.”

After exhaling deeply, and against his better judgment, he steps into the lobby. Brushing by several White people milling about, he notices a few of them squinting out of the soiled windows, their attention oddly fixed on the parking lot.

Not letting curiosity get the better of him, Winston continues on to the front desk.

The front desk attendant is anything but; she is a middle-aged White woman wearing bifocals that are as dirty as the windows and doors in the lobby. The closer he gets, the more he can see the filthy details of her bifocals. They are covered with smudges, fingerprints, and dust.

A look of disgust pours over his face.

Winston gingerly steps forward and says, "Ahhh...Hello? I'm looking for a room for one night. King-sized bed."

The attendant looks up at him, annoyed. She glances up briefly before returning her attention to her computer. Then, in a flippant manner, she says, "One-o-nine, plus tax. We only got one room for you, and it's in the back."

Raising an eyebrow, he asks, "In the back?"

She promptly responds, "Yes, and we got rules down in these parts."

Suddenly, the attendant bends down and retrieves a big, black weathered book, which appears to be an antique. She lobs the heavy book on the desk, causing a cloud of dust to billow into the air.

Adjusting her glasses, she begins to read aloud, "Rule number one…"

However, Winston's focus is interrupted as he notices a maid passing by. She is a dainty, attractive blonde woman dressed in a worn cleaning uniform. She stands before a vast mural adorning the wall near the elevator.

Winston devotes all of his attention to the mural, whose presence drowns out the attendant's incessant chatter. The mural depicts a controversial scene: numerous White individuals strolling through a park, passing by a Confederate statue.

In the backdrop, there stands an imposing, old clock tower atop an official-looking building. As Winston scrutinizes the mural, he discerns musical notes drifting through the air within the scene. Further along, other White figures in the painting are constructing train tracks, with a distant train approaching. A shiver runs down

Winston's spine as an eerie sensation envelops him.

The picture gives a dense presence of White people wearing colorful clothing. Winston is surprised to see in the crowd that there is a single Black man looking fearful. He is the one whistling, as the musical notes dangle from his lips. Shifting his attention away from the painting, Winston can sense the maid's gaze fixed upon him. When their eyes meet, he observes that she is blinking profusely. Winston tilts his head and looks at her wildly.

She slightly pulls down one of her white gloves to reveal that her hands are that of a Black person, leaving Winston visibly shaken. His reaction is immediate; he reaches into his pocket and retrieves a pill bottle. He pops one into his mouth, chews, and quickly swallows it. He can't tear his eyes away from the maid. At first, he thinks that he is hallucinating, but he isn't.

Observing Winston's response, the maid stops blinking, composes herself, and pulls her glove back up. She continues to clean as if nothing ever happened. Now the front desk attendant's voice takes center stage as she loudly continues to recite from her wretched tome, saying, "Rule number thirteen—"

He dismissively replies, "Yep! Whatever's in your Nigga Manual is cool with me. We're only going to be here for one night."

The attendant smacks her lips and slams the book closed.

Totally unbothered by Winston's words, she asks, "So it's two of y'all, huh?"

He looks her eye-to-eye and sharply replies, "Correct. Two. Human. People."

Winston looks back toward the maid, but she is gone. He hesitates for a moment, then hands the front desk attendant his credit card. She swiftly processes the transaction, tosses him the room keys, and slams his card onto the edge of the counter.

Winston remains oblivious to her rudeness as his attention is absorbed in scanning the lobby, where people wander about, some with smudged glasses. Even the TV screen appears filthy. He reaches over, retrieves his credit card and room pass, then exits the lobby, heading toward the parking lot.

As he walks back to the car, he briefly glances at the hotel, noticing that all the people who had been peering through the windows are now gone. Mumbling to himself, he says, "This place is weird as shit!" Meanwhile, Lori leans against the car door, listening to music and scrolling through her cell phone as she waits.

She checks-in her location with social media, and a blast of pings starts to go off. As she focuses on her phone, Winston yanks the door open, and her phone drops onto the gravel and cracks the entire face of the screen. Lori looks at Winston and angrily shouts in Mandarin, "Shénme tā mā de wēn sī dùn! What the fuck, Winston, you made me drop my phone!"

A crack of thunder can be heard in the distance.

He rushes around the car, saying, "Sorry, babe... But this is a shit, shower, and shave kinda place if you know what I mean? Let's get in there, do exactly that. Then get the fuck out first thing in the morning."

Lori bends down and picks up her phone. The screen blinks on and off. She can see that someone has messaged her, but it blinked too quickly for her to register anything. Winston helps her out of the car and kisses her in between grabbing the suitcases and bags. Out of breath, he says, "I'm sorry... I'll buy you a new one."

CHAPTER FOUR

As rain begins to drizzle from the darkened skies, Winston and Lori walk as briskly as they can back to the lobby. Upon entering, a hairy man with a bird-like nose and long arms holds out his hands. He never utters a word; he just carries their bags down the hall. With each galumphing footstep, they ascend down a hall until they reach the last door.

When they arrive, the strange-looking man turns to them and smiles with a devious grin, dropping their belongings unceremoniously.

Winston smiles back, forcing out the words, "Thank you," with a hint of a question mark at the end. The man turns and walks away until only faint thumping remains.

Lori lightens the mood with a joke, playfully singing, "Come on, 'it's only for one night,' in her best Luther Vandross voice."

Winston tries not to laugh. A skeptical smile forming on his face, as he inserts the key into the door. The lock clicks, and they step into the room, greeted by an atmosphere that seems frozen in a bygone era. The room bears visible signs of wear and neglect as if it has witnessed years of tears and struggles.

The furnishings, straight out of a time capsule from the early 1960s, stand as relics of a different era. The surfaces are drenched in worn Formica, the once vibrant patterns now faded with time. The upholstery on the chairs and bed appears scratchy to the touch, the fabric showing the scars of countless guests who came before. The wood furnishings, likely machine-molded, exude a tiredness that speaks of decades of use.

Then he notices the windows and remarks, “Of course, the windows are dirty too.”

Lori agrees, saying, “I see what you mean about the ‘shit, shower, and shave.’ But look on the bright side, they gave us complimentary tea and honey!”

Lori rushes over and picks up the jar, exclaiming, “And it looks so fancy!”

He shakes his head and sighs, “Number one... I’m not eating or drinking a damn thing in this place. Number two, honey ain’t nothing but bee spit with outstanding marketing. Nope!”

Lori sarcastically waves her hand at him, saying, “On that note, I’m going to bed.” She undresses and peels the covers back. Winston shuts the overhead light off and gets in the bed. Lori falls asleep quickly. A little while later, Winston turns on his nightstand lamp.

He looks over to Lori to see if she’s asleep; she is.

Glancing over, he eyes a TV remote control on the nightstand. He looks across the room and raises his brow at the television, mumbling, “Geez...how old is this place?”

Grabbing the remote, he feels something wiry in his hand. Squinting, he finds a small wad of short black curly hairs stuck to it. Disgusted, he yelps “Oh...My...God! This is the shit that I be talking about. How do you not…”

He scowls. “Apparently, the chick with them black-ass hands ain’t been cleaning in here. Ewww!”

Frantically, he shakes the remote and reaches into Lori’s purse on her nightstand. He pulls out a few tissues, wipes the remote off, and tosses the tissue across the room. Smiling now, he says, “Alrighty then.” Then he clicks the remote. The television screen comes on, but it’s nothing but snow and wavy lines. Winston continues to click until a clear channel appears. Surprisingly, music from a vintage talk show begins to play.

He squints at the program, as it resembles a scene straight out of a vintage Johnny Carson show. He thinks, “This is so retro,” as the intro plays in black and white, with bold white letters overlaying the host and a guest.

Winston whispers, “The Dell Ferrell Show.” The title then fades away, revealing the host: a dapper middle-aged man with alabaster skin, slicked-back black hair, and dressed in a crisp dark suit with a pencil-thin black tie.

“Yeah, dude is kinda smooth-looking,” he comments.

The studio audience was filled with cheering and clapping White faces dressed in 1950s fashions. The host greeted the camera and the audience with a warm smile and mouthed pleasantries.

Winston finds himself oddly entertained by the show, but his full engagement is sparked when he sees Mr. Ferrell’s guest. Seated across from him is an attractive Black woman with a massive afro, sporting a denim jacket and pants adorned with various pins and buttons conveying messages and images of Black Power. She sits stoically in her chair, grimacing at Dell and the audience.

Dell Ferrell chirps, “Hello...Hello...Hello! It’s great to be here. What a wonderful audience we have tonight! Well, tonight we have a special guest.”

The audience grumbles and chatters. The guest scans the audience with a scowl on her face. Dell pulls a cigarette from an open pack, lights it, and takes a pull. He blows smoke out towards the audience and raises his hand making a waving motion to simmer them down.

"Calm yourselves, you know that every now and again, the 'Dell Ferrell Show' likes to see how the other half lives," he belts out. "It's important to do a little housekeeping - if you know what I mean."

The audience quiets down, and Dell turns to his guest, continuing, "As I was saying, we have a special guest today."

"Her name is Saturn Pride—."

With much chagrin, she cuts him off before he can mangle her name and corrects him, "That's Saddura. S-a-d-d-u-r-a. Saddura."

Embarrassed, Dell responds, "Oh yes, of course. That doesn't roll off the tongue easily, does it, ladies and gents?"

Dell looks at the audience and laughs, with the audience joining in.

Dell continues, "How about, just for the interview, we call you 'Sadie'? That's a good ole gal's name. We like that name. Isn't that right?"

Dell looks at the audience and broadens his smile. He extends his arms and claps his hands toward the audience, and they respond with enthusiastic applause.

Saddura shakes her head from side to side in disgust, causing the audience to quiet down.

Dell hurriedly begins the interview, saying, "So Sadie, we've heard all about your protests for Black Rights, Voting Rights, and Fair Housing. Those are some doozies. However, slavery is over and you people can go and do as you please. America has moved past that unpleasantness. We don't need free labor anymore, our country is in the black! Isn't that right, ladies and gentlemen?"

The audience erupts in applause and conversation. A few audience members begin to shout, "Yes! That's right! Yeah! We work hard to pay our bills!"

Saddura lets out an exasperated sigh before unleashing a measured but scathing response, "America can't let it go...because enslavement is not just about economics or a chain around your neck. Enslaving others is about the four-letter spiritual illness you people suffer from. It speaks to your core like a mother who sings to her baby in the womb. Enslavement is ultimately about White laziness, entitlement, hubris, and your collective fetish for abuse."

Dell's eyes beam as he races to put out his cigarette in the ashtray. The members of the audience gasp and grumble in unison.

Winston excitedly leans forward with his mouth open, cheering, "What the hell! Shit...she gotta be thirsty 'cuz she ate them crackers up!"

Still holding the remote, he pressed the buttons, turning the volume up. Lori sighs in her sleep and turns slightly, opening her eyes. The television makes a crackling sound and shuts off.

He frantically shouts, "No…No...No...No!"

Repeatedly he presses the power button on the remote control, flips it over, and gives it a firm smack. He then jumps out of bed and tries to manually turn the television on but with no success. Frustrated, he bangs on the top and sides of the TV.

Lori, slurring her words and still mostly asleep, asks, "What's happening?"

Winston quickly returns to his side of the bed.

Stuttering, "I...I don't know. I was watching this show and then boom. Nothing!"

Lori pats him reassuringly on the arm and says, "It's been a long day. Just go to sleep."

He stares at Lori and then back at the television. He drops the remote on the nightstand, turns off the lamp, lies down with a thump, and goes to sleep.

It begins to rain outside, picking up steam as the night progresses. Through the dirty windows, the rain begins to fall heavier. Thunder and lightning follow. The darkness of the room looks like an abyss, except for the occasional flashes of lightning.

As Winston and Lori sleep, cracks of thunder sound throughout the room, revealing that the bed is completely surrounded by many large, ominous-looking men wearing white hoodie jackets. The hoods are pointy and pulled down, obscuring their faces. They are dirty and wet, looking down at the couple.

The lightning continues to flash a couple more times. The group is now bent over and taking turns touching Winston. Winston makes a distressed sound and groggily opens his eyes.

More lightning flashes follow. Winston is roused awake by the noise and what feels like tentacles touching him. He blinks several times and then sits up straight in bed.

As he looks around, he realizes the room is empty. Glancing down, he murmurs, "What's that?"

He feels his chest and examines his hand, which is wet and slightly sticky. Too tired to move, he wipes his hand on the sheet and then lies back down to sleep.

In the morning, Lori and Winston wake up, facing each other. She coyly whispers, "Hey, you. Did you get any sleep?"

Winston yawns and responds, "Yes... Maybe... I think?"

Lori lifts her head and rests it on her hand, asking, "What do you mean, you think?"

He points out, "I woke up in a cold, sticky sweat. But it's not just sweat; I'm soaking wet. When have I ever done that?"

Lori playfully jokes, "Well, it's certainly nothing that a hot shower can't fix." Lori then stands up next to the bed, pulling the blanket to wrap herself in.

Lori has a curious look on her face. "Babe, did you go out last night?" She looks around the room and notices that the honey jar is empty on the tray. "And I see you changed your mind about the tea."

Winston looks in her direction, perplexed. "Out? Yeah... No. It was raining cats and dogs. Besides, where would I go in this creepy-ass town? And what's this about tea?"

She points to the tray with the beverages and replies, "Well, the jar of honey is empty." She looks at the blanket covering her. There is a plastic spoon covered in honey stuck to it. She picks up the spoon and holds it up, asking, "Why is this on the bed?"

With a troubling expression, she drops the spoon on the floor. Looking down, she discovers something else: puddles and shoe trails of murky water.

Winston eyeballs Lori wildly. Lori continues, "And why are there wet, muddy shoe prints all over the floor?"

Winston sits up and catches a glimpse of the floor, noticing wet, multiple muddy shoe prints lining his side of the bed as well.

In a shout of frustration, he exclaims, "What in the entire fuck is this?"

He jumps up and paces around the bed in a panic, frantically searching for his pill bottle on the nightstand. It's gone!

He begins to chant in a frenzy, "This isn't happening... This isn't happening!"

Winston's heart races and panic sets in. He searches around the nightstand, in the drawer, and on the bed. He even bends down frantically to check under the bed.

There are no pills to be found.

Lori steps closer to Winston and says, "Calm down, babe. We'll find them."

Winston looks up, clearly experiencing a full-blown anxiety attack.

Lori, breathing heavily, adds, "Do you think someone was in our room?"

She walks to the window, which appears wet and smudged from the inside. She mumbles, "And why is the window so dirty anyway?"

She backs away from the bed, positioning herself against the nearest wall. Winston, still breathing heavily, starts packing up their belongings.

Nervously, Winston utters, "Oh, no, no, no. Forget what I said about the 'shit, shower, and shave.' We're leaving right now!"

Lori desperately rummages through her bag and retrieves a shirt, hastily putting it on. She does the same with her pants, tears welling up in her eyes as she asks, "What's happening right now?"

Winston quickly gets dressed, his movements hurried and tense. In his packing frenzy, he accidentally grabs the TV remote control and packs it among his things.

They hurry out of the room and slam the door behind them. Lori goes up to Winston and asks, "Did you find your meds?" Winston, screaming in frustration, replies, "No... They're gone! Just gone!"

Lori takes both of his hands in hers and peers into his eyes. She takes a deep breath and calmly reassures him, saying, "Just breathe. I promise... It will be okay."

They gather their belongings and swiftly exit the room.

The pair hurriedly make their way down the hall. Lori accidentally drops a bag but quickly retrieves it and catches up to Winston, who continues toward the lobby. As they pass the elevator and the mural on the wall, Winston suddenly stops, his eyes fixed on the mural, particularly the Black man whistling.

Lori rushes past him, then abruptly halts and retraces her steps to join him in looking at the mural. However, she focuses her attention on the music notes. After a moment, she snaps back to the urgency of them getting out of there.

She shouts, "Winston, let's get out of here!" She walks away quickly while Winston remains transfixed.

Several people in the mural are depicted as pale White, but they have jet-black hands. He eventually tears his eyes away, rushes over to Lori, and tosses the room key onto the front desk as they hurry towards the front door.

The front desk attendant smiles and says, "See ya' next time!"

Winston frowns and replies without looking back, "Not if we see you first!" As the couple enters the parking lot, they are met with torrential rain. They spot several White men wearing wet and dingy white zip-up hoodies wandering in clusters throughout the parking lot.

These men are large, hunched, and unmistakably corn-fed. Their hoods are pulled low over their faces as they communicate with one another in a low, murmured tone, like a jumbled chant.

One of the men has a thick twine rope hanging from his overall pocket. Winston whispers, "What is it with White men and ropes?"

Suddenly, a low, resonating, maniacal Joker-type laughter emanates from the woods.

In a low and hurried tone, Winston comments, "What in the Vincent Price... Thriller Night was that!"

Terrified, Winston and Lori look at the men and assess the distance to their car. Winston grabs Lori's hand, and they both begin to run towards the car.

Winston rushes to the driver's side door while Lori heads for the passenger side. Both of them remain on edge, scanning their surroundings nervously. The groups of men are slowly closing in on them, and the mumbling grows louder.

Winston frantically pats himself down, searching for the keys.

Lori, terrified, screams, "Winston... hurry... hurry... hurry!"

He retrieves the keys from his pocket but accidentally drops them on the ground. He quickly picks them up and presses the fob to unlock the doors, causing the car to chirp.

He shouts, "Get in! Get in!"

Lori jumps into the passenger seat, and Winston tosses their bags into the back before leaping into the driver's seat. The headlights flash on, and the car peels off. Lori glances out the back window, and the mob stands together, watching the back of their car as it speeds away.

When they had reached a safe distance, Lori exclaimed, "What in the name of sweet baby Jesus was that?"

Winston responds with composure, "That, Lori, is what we call a 'Welcome Wagon.' I guess we know who paid us a visit last night!"

Taken aback, Lori replies, "Oh my God, just keep driving!"

Lori, still gawking in her side-view mirror, pleads, "Go faster; they might be searching for us in their pickup truck."

Winston does his best to navigate through the heavy rain, responding, "We can't keep driving like this. We're going to get ourselves killed."

Lori begins to fiddle with the radio, saying, "Let me put something on to keep the adrenaline pumping."

She settles on a station, and the next thing Winston hears is Adele's "Hello." Lori nervously starts to hum the melody as Winston glances between her and the road repeatedly.

He sarcastically asks, "Are you insane? This ain't no goddamn getaway music. Give me my phone."

Lori hands him his phone from the console. Winston manipulates the phone with one hand while driving with the other.

He utters, "Ah-ha! Here we go", loud music starts playing. It's "B.O.B" by OutKast. As they speed over train tracks at a crossing, the car thumps and bumps along the tracks.

In the year 1755, within the confines of a weathered log cabin cocooned in the heart of a dense forest, sits Hanna-May, an elderly brown-skinned Black woman. Her once-dark, kinky hair had now begun to show strands of gray. She's humming a tune that blends elements of somber jazz fusion and traditional Negro hymns, her focus entirely on the large canvas before her. The canvas is propped up by a makeshift easel, and it depicts a scene of a slave ship disembarking Black individuals into a gathering of awaiting White individuals. As Hanna-May meticulously applies her brushstrokes, she pays special attention to the vivid portrayal of blood flowing from the enslaved figures. It's worth noting that while Hanna-May's hands are dark in complexion, small white patches of skin have emerged on her wrists.

CHAPTER FIVE

As Lori sleeps, Winston looks for another place to spend the next couple of days. Not wanting to wake Lori, he pulls into a parking lot near a grove of trees. A little while later, Lori begins to yawn and stretch, waking from her sleep.

The windows are fogged as Lori turns to Winston, asking, "Where are we now?"

He responds, "I don't know. I saw a house and this lot from the road and pulled in. It looked safe enough to get some shut-eye."

Lori holds up her phone with its darkened screen. "Darn… my phone still won't come on."

Winston picks up his phone and types on it. "We're in Alabama now." Winston switches on the wipers while Lori uses her sleeve to wipe the moisture off the passenger's side window.

He blurts, "Yep… this is the place I saw. It was so yellow it lit up the night like a flashlight!"

As they peer out of the windshield, they smile at the beautiful bright yellow Victorian home trimmed with a black finish. In the yard swings a sign that reads "Bee-Bee's B&B."

Lori remarks, "Looks harmless enough, kinda like a gingerbread house."

Winston side-eyes Lori and replies, "Said the fly entering the spider's web." He grins.

She smiles and utters, "Look, it says Bee Bee's B&B... Anybody that would name their business that is corny, not crazy." They both chuckle.

Lori's attitude changes as she turns empathetic. Looking lovingly at Winston, she says, "Sorry about your pills."

He replies, "Yeah... I have to get a refill asap!"

Lori adds, "I hate that you have to take them in the first place."

He concurs, "Yeah, it's been quite a while."

Lori inquires, "Do you recall what your diagnosis was back then?"

Winston comically huffs and replies, "Well, that's something I can never forget. They call it O.D.D."

Lori mumbles, "O.D.D... O.D.D? Wait... I remember learning about this in school. O.D.D means 'Oppositional Defiant Disorder.' The symptoms, as they explained it, include a frequent and ongoing pattern of anger, irritability, arguing, and defiance towards authority figures."

Winston chuckles, "Well... I don't have any of those."

Lori looks suspicious. "No... you don't."

He shrugs, "However, I do have a host of other medical issues like frequent dizziness, tachycardia, blackouts, and overall anxiety. I guess…it works for that too! I never thought to look into it since it always worked for me."

"To be honest, it sounds sort of made up," Lori says. "However, this is a conversation for another day. So, let's go on up in this Gingerbread House and get something to eat and some sleep. Then we can take care of your refill."

Giggling, he replies, "Sounds like a plan! I'll grab the gear while you get us checked in."

He pulls a credit card from his wallet and passes it to Lori as she steps out.

Lori gets out of the car and looks around the area. Troubled, she says, "This place looks to be vacant, too. That's strange."

Looking out the window to the sky, Winston disagrees, "Nah… it's probably just all that rain. We're the only idiots out here driving in it. Don't worry, maybe they'll have some cookies waiting for us."

Lori shrugs it off and heads up the stairs of the B&B. Winston unloads the bags.

A train whistle blows from a nearby train line.

Before Winston can close the trunk, an all-white rabbit with black paws hops out.

The rabbit stops and looks directly at Winston. They stare at each other for a moment, and then the rabbit turns and hops away. Winston lingers, his head tilted to the side, then eventually walks away.

Lori is in awe of the decor in the lobby. It mimics the exterior of the home, striped in yellow and black with white accents. A low, calming melody plays throughout the space. As Lori progresses, she sees a young, pretty front desk attendant talking to a flamboyantly dressed Black man.

She stops short of the desk, standing respectfully behind the man. While she stands there, she admires his black extravagant suit with a turquoise exaggerated bow tie and a string of black pearls. She notices that he even has bright turquoise nail polish to match his turquoise shoes.

The man at the counter is equally enchanted by the surroundings, breaks into a smile, and takes in the lobby with a sweeping glance. He then leans casually on the counter and exclaims, "Yaasssss... Yas! I'm feeling this place. It's antiquated but chic, you know? This will do nicely."

The front desk attendant, identified by her badge reading "Harlow," politely interrupts the man, saying, "Sir... ish?"

The man bucks his eyes and clutches a loose band of black pearls dangling from his neck.

Harlow shrinks, and says, "Ah... Sir, could you please refrain from leaning on the counter? It's quite old, and we want to preserve it. Also, I'm sorry, but may I ask for your name again?"

In response, he straightens up defiantly and declares loudly, "I'm gonna give it to you, one mo'- gen'. It's Quizzie." He rapidly spells it out with his index finger to emphasize: Q-U-I-Z-Z-I-E.

Harlow frantically searches the computer while Quizzie mumbles sarcastically, "Guess my name doesn't ring a bell in these parts."

Harlow hesitates but then says, "Okay, I found it. Can you please take a seat over there?" She points to a seating area near the entrance.

Quizzie purses his lips and replies, "Mmmm... Hmmmmm." He snuffs his nose at Harlow and walks away.

As he walks away, Lori steps forward. Quizzie breezes by her, grinning and waving with his right hand. Lori recognizes him from television and feels giddy to see him in person.

Lori hears someone speaking and looks in that direction. It's the attendant announcing, "Hello, my name is Harlow, and welcome to Bee Bee's B&B!"

Lori turns her attention toward the desk, giddily smiling. She had just met a social media darling.

Excitedly, she yelps, "Oh my God! That's... that's Quizzie, the Food Dude!"

Harlow stares at Lori coldly.

Lori looks into Harlow's eyes more closely and notices that she is wearing contact lenses, which appear to be clear with spots of brown on them.

Lori shakes off her unease and returns to the conversation, saying, "Hello! My name is Lori. Nice to meet you. Do you have any rooms available?"

Harlow attempts to respond but is distracted by Winston walking through the door. Struggling, Winston grunts, "Hey, babe... do they have a room?"

He peeks at Quizzie, who is sitting in the lobby area, flipping through a magazine.

He notices the stranger's vibrant attire and colorful nails as well.

Winston struggles forward with the bags and comes to stand next to Lori. Lori smiles at Winston and then at Harlow.

Lori attempts to get Harlow's attention, saying, "You were saying?"

Harlow, with frustration, snarls, "We have no MOOR rooms. Buzz... Buzz."

Lori is taken aback and asks, "Excuse me, what does that mean?"

Harlow begins to scream, "I said, we have no "MOORRR" rooms! Buzz... Buzz!"

Lori has a cross and also a perplexed look on her face. She steps back. Winston drops the bags, rushing to her aid, and angrily questions, "Chick…What is wrong with you? Where's your manager?"

Harlow aggressively demands, "Sir, I need you to calm down!"

He charges back, "Just go and get your manager!"

Harlow rushes away from the front desk and down the hall.

Just then, an older White man with piercing blue eyes dressed in a bellhop's uniform walks over to the pair. The bellhop moves closer to Winston and whispers, "Don't get angry. Apologize and tell them that you'll take the room in the back."

Taken aback, Winston asks, "Wait... What? You're kidding right?"

The bellhop is insistent. "Tell them that you'll take the room in the back, or you'll never get out of here."

Angry now, Winston shouts, "Are you serious?"

The bellhop's eyes pan down, and he slightly extends his hand. He peels back the glove on his right hand. Winston's eyes grow large as he follows the bellhop's White wrist to his dark-complexioned hands.

Lori peeks over their shoulders at the unbelievable sight. Suddenly, they hear chatter and the clicking of high-heeled shoes coming in the distance.

The bellhop looks around cautiously and slightly pulls up his hat, revealing a large patch of black kinky hair surrounded by oily, blondish stringy hair. Lori gasps, and Winston whispers wildly, "What the fuck?"

The Bellhop quickly pulls his cap back down and rushes to stand by the front desk.

The chatter is getting louder, coming closer. An older, heavy-set White woman wearing a bright yellow floral dress stomps to the desk with Harlow in tow. She has bright red, tight, curly hair and is heavily freckled.

Laughing rudely, she said, "I see what ya' mean, Harlow. We got us a couple of real-life busy bees here."

Lori attempts to speak, but Winston pulls her back. Winston speaks up sarcastically, replying, "Yes. Well, Buzz... Buzz!"

She snorts, "Buzz... Buzz indeed. My name is Bertha Bellows, and I'm the proprietor of this establishment."

She jumps right to business, "I hear ya' looking for a room?"

Ignoring the initial complaint, Winston smirks, "Yes, ma'am, we are. We don't need anything special." He mellows out and says, "Actually, we'll just take a room in the back."

Winston looks at the bellhop and winks, then he looks back to Bertha.

She quips, "Great! That's real good." Bertha opens several drawers in the desk. She pulls out a pair of filthy glasses and shoves them on her face.

She continues, "Ah, that's better."

Winston and Lori exchange looks of incredulity.

She goes on, "Here we go. Room 108-B. It's a sub-room in the back, downstairs. Belly, get them to their room."

The bellhop happily replies, "Yes, Ma'am. Right away."

Lori blurts out, "What about…"

Winston abruptly grabs her hand tightly, and she stops talking.

Bertha cautions, "We only take cash from you!"

Winston takes a deep breath, releases Lori's hand, and pulls out his wallet. Asking, "How much?"

She replies, "One hundred seventy-nine dollars and ninety-nine cents, plus tax, and one hundred dollars for incidentals."

Winston and Lori step away from the group and whisper back and forth. Lori pulls some cash from her purse and gives it to him.

He hands the money to Bertha, and she hands him a room key.

Winston then asks, "What about our receipt?"

Bertha frowns, “We’ll email it to you.”

Lori chimes in, saying, “But you don’t have our email—”

Winston cuts her off, “That’s fine. Thank you so much!”

The bellhop waits for them near the lobby’s hallway. Still holding their bags, he leads them down the hall.

With an insistent look, the bellhop signals the couple to follow him down the corridor.

Lori asks, “What’s going on?”

The bellhop cautiously places his finger over his lips and says, “Shh… Shh.”

Winston and Lori walk behind the bellhop, keeping pace. As they trail him, Winston sees strange art on the wall, similar to the murals that he and Lori saw at the other hotel.

The people are dressed differently than the Jekyll mural, and everyone is pale White, except for one Black woman whistling a tune. Winston slows down and looks closer at some of the White people in the painting.

Several of the White men’s hands are also jet black.

Lori stops and looks as well, saying, “Huh…” and begins to quietly hum the notes on the mural.

She then mentions, “The melody doesn’t make any sense. The notes are like a disconnected fugue.”

Winston whispers, “What’s a fugue?”

She answers, “When a composer uses interweaving repetitive elements instead of a sensible melody that you can follow. The notes read more like a musical conversation than a song.”

Winston nods his head while still enthralled in the painting, responding dismissively, “Right…right.” He pauses for a moment then asks, “But do you see this strange art? Even Basquiat would question this.”

Lori begins to walk away, muttering under her breath, "Winston. Winston, come on."

He pulls himself away and catches up.

They arrive at a spiral stairwell and descend to a lower level. A thick stench hangs in the air. Lori and Winston reflexively cover their noses in response to the smell.

The bellhop continues to move down the short spiral staircase as if he were accustomed to the malodorous scent. Winston and Lori move cautiously because the stairwell appears to narrow the farther they descend. They are now shoulder-to-shoulder with the stair's railing and the walls.

Winston frowns. "What in the Devil's asshole is that smell?"

Finally, they reach a darkened landing. The corridor is dimly lit, and only one door is visible on the left. The trio approaches it, and it reads 108-B.

Winston exclaims angrily, "Nah, man. Just no! What is this... the boiler room?"

The Bellhop places all the bags and suitcases on the floor at their feet.

The bellhop interrupts him, stuttering, "Mr. Winston, let's discuss this in the room. Please, just not here."

Winston shouts, "Room... by room, do you mean this broom closet?"

The bellhop begs, "Sir, please."

Winston waves him off. "Whatever, man."

Lori huffs, grabs the keys from the bellhop, and pushes open the door. Winston scans the room, spotting an older-model TV and a queen-sized bed flanked by two nightstands. They step closer for a better look. The bellhop sets the bags down and closes the door.

Lori shares her verdict, "It's not extremely horrible."

Winston snorts, “Yeah, it’s just regular horrible. Now that that’s out of the way…”

Winston sharply stares at the bellhop, his tone demanding, “What the Hell is going on? What’s with those weird-ass paintings in the hall? And what’s up with your damn hands, dude? It’s some funky shit going on with the White people in these parts. Can’t say that I’m in a rush to find out what it is.”

The bellhop walks toward the couple and says, “We don’t have a lot of time. Don’t unpack, keep your door locked, and don’t... I repeat, do not eat anything. Remember Persephone.”

Concerned, Lori asks, “I’m sorry... Who is Persephone?”

The bellhop rushes to leave. “I have to go. But my hands are who I really am,” he says. “Pay attention to the paintings; they will lead the way. Leave in the morning exactly at 4:33 a.m. Not a moment sooner and not a minute later. And stay away from the train tracks!”

Puzzled, Winston inquires, “Train tracks?”

Then the bellhop suddenly darts out of the room and slams the door shut.

Lori asks, “What in the world was that... and why are you making fun of that man’s condition?”

Winston raises a brow, “What condition?”

Lori replies, “His Vitiligo.”

Winston shakes his head, explaining, “Michael Jackson had Vitiligo. That bellhop has something else going on, but it for damn sure ain’t no Vitiligo.”

Lori looks at him with pity in her eyes and sits down next to Winston on the bed. “What do you think of those paintings?”

Winston quickly replies, “Crazy! I mean, who paints shit like that?”

Lori insists, “The musical arrangement doesn’t make sense.”

“Babe, it doesn’t have to make sense. They were just painting pictures, not creating a playlist. Try not to read too much into it.”

Then out of nowhere, there’s a knock at the door. They both exchange concerned glances, then cautiously turn their attention toward the door. Winston calls out, “Hello?”

A man’s voice rings out from the other side of the door, “Hello, sir. We’ve brought you some complimentary brunch. May I come in?”

Winston’s face goes pale from fright. “Ah... no. We had a long drive. We’re just going to turn in,” he stammers.

The man’s voice grows insistent. “I understand, but you really should eat something. We have one of the best chefs in Alabama. Open the door; you will love the spread I have.”

Winston panics, looks at Lori, and motions that he’s out of answers. He repeats, louder this time, “Like I said, we’re dead tired. Maybe later.”

The doorknob begins to rattle violently.

Winston rushes over and pushes his back against the door, shouting as he leans against it, “OK… OK! Just leave it at the door. We’ll get it in a few minutes.”

There’s a loud thump and a rattle in the hall with clunky footsteps fading away.

“Yeah, these people are crazy! We gotta leave.”

Lori starts to move toward the door.

Winston stops her and whispers, “We can’t leave, not right now. The bellhop said that we can’t leave until early morning.”

Lori questions, “I still don’t understand why not... and HOW early?”

Winston sighs. “He said exactly 4:33 a.m., and it didn’t sound optional. You heard what he said about Persephone and to NOT eat the food.”

Lori wears a confused expression on her face.

“Persephone… food?”

And then they both look at each other, see the shock of recognition, and shout simultaneously, “PERSEPHONE!”

Winston picks up his phone and begins an internet search while Lori looks over his shoulder.

He begins to read aloud.

“Persephone knew that if she ate or drank anything in the underworld, she would have to stay there forever. But before she leaves, Hades offers Persephone one last thing to eat – a ripe, blood-red pomegranate. Looking him in the eye, Persephone took six seeds and ate them. But, because Persephone had eaten six pomegranate seeds, it was decided that for six months of each year, she must return to the underworld with Hades.”

Lori gasps.

They tip over to the door and press their ears against it. Winston opens the door to see a food tray with a silver cloche. He quickly lifts the top to reveal an array of fruits, sliced meats, cheeses, and dark breads, among other things. Winston looks a little closer to see an opened jar of honey dripping on the plate of food. He drops the lid and slams the door shut.

“Uh...uh...uh. More honey. White people love that stuff!”

Disturbed, Lori says, “Babe...they literally gave us a pomegranate? This has to be a joke. Should we listen to him?”

“I don’t know,” Winston replies, “but the bellhop and the housekeeper at the other place are clearly White, but they have black hands. This guy even has a patch of nappy hair. So, something unsavory is going on.”

Winston's cell phone rings. He quickly answers, "Hello."

On the other end, he can hear his sister Chloe barking orders to someone. She redirects her attention to Winston. "Hey, baby brother, how's the pilgrimage going?"

Winston pauses before he responds, "Chloe, I'm so glad to hear your voice. To be honest, it's a little more than I bargained for. Just do me a favor."

Sidelining Winston, Chloe continues to fuss, "No…not over there. Put that on the truck! You break it, you bought it!"

Winston, stammering, says, "I…I can't talk about it right now, but keep your phone on. I'll call you back soon."

Chloe asks, "Okay. You sure you're alright?"

Winston shrugs. "Yeah, we're good. Just a little tired, that's all."

With worry in her voice, Chloe replies, "Okay, be careful out there."

Winston hangs up the phone and sighs.

He turns to Lori, his medication is suddenly on his mind. "No matter what's going on tomorrow, I gotta get a refill. We'll leave here early in the morning. We have to get to Tennessee ASAP."

Lori suggests, "I've noticed that you've been taking those more than usual. When we make it to Chicago, let's find a more holistic way to treat your condition."

Winston plants his chin in his hand and shakes his head. Lori picks up her phone and heads to the bathroom.

Lori creeps into the bathroom with caution. As she surveys the room, it becomes evident that neglect has taken its toll. Dirty, golden floor tiles greet her, and tattered wallpaper clings desperately to the walls. The toilet, bizarrely painted white with flat wall paint, is notably odd, as evidenced by a rusted paint bucket hidden behind the bowl.

Despite the fact that the wallpaper was peeling off the walls, Lori thought that it felt out of place against the backdrop because it depicted a beautiful scene of woods, trees, and bushes on a golden background.

Lori decides to use her index finger to rub the textured wallpaper gently, asking, "Who put you here?" Then she turns and pulls the stained shower curtain back and turns on the shower.

Brown water sprays out unexpectedly, accompanied by a malodorous stench, causing her to quickly cover her nose and gag in disgust.

The water eventually begins to clear, and she removes her hand from her nose as the smell dissipates. She shakes her head and mumbles, "Never again!"

While the water runs, she sits on the toilet and checks to see if she can get her phone to work. The cracked screen blinks on and off then stays on. She yells, "Winston, my phone is on!"

Realizing that he can't hear her, she continues to look through it.

The screen display shows that she has forty-seven Facebook messages and twenty-two missed text messages.

She opens a text message from a friend, Stacey.

Stacey's text reads: "What are you guys doing in Jekyll?"

Lori opens a second text message.

Stacey continues: "My friend stopped through there last year, and we never saw her again!"

Lori tries to open a third message, but the phone cuts off. She squints at the phone's badly cracked screen.

"What the hell?" Lori yells at her phone.

She tries to turn the phone on again with no luck, then lays her phone on the sink and gets in the shower.

CHAPTER SIX

In the next room, Winston lies sprawled across the bed, his face contorting with pain as his stomach growls incessantly. His hand moves instinctively to his midsection, offering it a gentle, soothing rub. With a wry grin, he mutters to himself, "I know one thing... I'm hungrier than a hostage, but first things first."

Grabbing his cell phone, he begins to search for doctor's offices in Chattanooga, Tennessee. Just then, he finds what he is looking for. He quickly dials the number and waits. A voice on the other end crackles to life, and Winston clears his throat before speaking, "Hello... I would like to make an appointment to see a doctor for a refill. No, I'm not a current patient."

The voice on the line is kind yet inquisitive, probing for more information. Winston's tone grows frustrated as he explains further, "No, ma'am, I can't call my doctor; he's back in Atlanta. I'm on the road. I need to see a doctor before I can get another refill. The prescription's name is Zencitravmasi."

As he awaits the response on the other end, his mind races, and his fingers drum nervously on the edge of the bed. The voice, now sympathetic, inquires about the milligram dosage, leaving Winston momentarily stumped. Until he remembers that he keeps an old bottle label in his wallet.

He reaches into his wallet and retrieves a folded, weathered paper. “It’s 500mg, 90-count,” he replies, the words escaping his lips like a lifeline.

Listening to the voice on the phone, he leans forward, his voice filled with elation, “I’ll take whatever you’ve got, but it has to be tomorrow at 4:30; that works for me! Okay, Thanks!”

With those words, Winston takes a deep breath, a sense of relief washing over him. He knows that tomorrow is going to be a better day.

Winston clicks the phone off and searches the internet for a restaurant that’s on the way to Tennessee. He scrolls and begins to laugh heartily, reading out loud, “Papa Bear’s Bar-B-Cue. Sounds like they serve potato salad with their ribs. I’ll bet there ain’t a Hotlink in the house!”

While Winston keeps himself occupied in search of food, Lori slowly exits the shower and wraps herself in the cleanest towel she can find. She retrieves lotion from her bag and begins to apply it to her body while facing the wall. She slows down and stares at the wallpaper.

Suddenly, she stops applying the lotion and moves closer. She can’t believe her eyes; she sees silhouettes of African-American people hidden behind trees and shrubbery in the scenes depicted on the wallpaper.

The longer she stares, the more she can discern tiny musical notes and short phrases camouflaged within the scenery. All the words appear in different handwriting styles, seemingly providing some form of direction.

"It's the Fugue notes again," she whispers, then raises her voice as she reads the words on the wallpaper. "Atlanta, Alabama, Tennessee, Kentucky, Indiana, Chicago."

She pauses briefly before continuing, "Mississippi, Tennessee, Kentucky, West Virginia, Maryland, New York."

Her voice trembles as she reads the next part.

"Don't eat the food. Don't drink the water. Don't go in the woods. Follow the Bellhop. Stay in the room. No MOOR room at the inn. No MOOR room at the inn. No MOOR room at the inn."

As she reads, the wallpaper seems to come alive with the silhouettes sneaking and running from tree to tree, hiding from bush to bush, like a moving film reel. The sounds of melancholic Jazz Fusion mix with Negro Hymns, accompanied by the clicking noise of a camera reel running.

Then, abruptly, the motion and sounds come to a halt.

Lori's body shudders, jolting back to the stark reality of the moment. Her heart races, with beats resonating through her chest. Still in disbelief of what she just witnessed, she hurries and collects her belongings, determined to put some distance between herself and the unsettling events. She then makes her way into the adjoining room where Winston awaits. Looking back at the bathroom door as she paces away, she nervously says, "Oh my God, Babe, there's some weird shit on the walls in there."

Winston continues to scroll on his phone, chuckling as he inquires, "Is it murderous muddy-mumble mob weird, or White people with black hands and nappy hair weird, or being held captive in the bowels of a gingerbread house Hell weird? Cause honestly, I can't tell anymore."

With deadpan eyes, Lori shouts, "This isn't funny! I swear I saw the wallpaper move and heard sounds. This is crazy!"

Looking up at Lori, Winston questions, "Are you high?"

She responds in a serious tone, "I'm serious!"

He sits up straight and says, "Keep in mind, I just saw the weirdest cases of vitiligo I've ever seen. In my book, it's just a regular Tuesday in a Black person's world." Lori is now dressed in a long T-shirt, black leggings, and white socks, asking, "Are we on this again?"

Sarcastically, Winston replies, "On what?"

"You know what...this Black-people-against-the-world thing."

He angrily claps back, "I don't see you losing your mind after reading the crazy shit you see on gas station bathroom walls. And baby, I'm here to tell you, that's when you should be scared. The only reason that you're pitching a bitch now is because you're being directly affected now."

Lori walks to the bed, pulls the covers back, and gets in, saying, "That's not true."

"The hell it ain't! Black people get assaulted and killed every day just for being Black. You see that shit on TV and you flick the channel like it wasn't nothing. Then, when I get stressed about it, you know what your remedy is?"

He pauses and then blurts out, "A blow job or some ass!"

Lori angrily speaks in Mandarin, "N gè wángbā dà!" [You son of a bitch!]

Winston gets out of bed and moves around the room, yelling as he goes.

"Nah...don't start that native tongue shit either. When Asians get assaulted or killed by these homegrown terrorists, y'all make the world stop and pay attention. The next thing we see is y'all on TV at the state capital. Y'all got a guest seat in Congress or you meeting with the President. Your protection is mandatory!"

He pauses and takes a deep breath before he goes on.

"And you know why? Fuckin' gradation!"

Lori looks at him with a pinched look on her face, asking with her voice cracking, "Gradation?"

Winston aggressively nods his head up and down.

"Uh-huh…yeah. It's levels to this racism shit. You see, here's the shade white...all the way up here."

He raises his hand flat over his head but as he speaks he lowers his hand. He went on.

"You got your stark white, pale white, peach white, and pink white."

He continues to lower his hand.

"Now we are falling into cream white, and tusk white. Now we're on to the yellow tones. That's where you and your people come in."

Lori looks at him shocked, shouting, "Winston!"

Her reaction didn't deter him.

"Actually, I can stop right here. Cause after yellow, it's a shit show. The Tans, Browns, and Blacks are woefully irrelevant to, you know, everybody. It's funny because you guys barely made the cut. But you align yourselves with them anyway, despite knowing that there are cuts being made."

She starts to cry.

Looking at her, his demeanor softens, and he sits on the bed next to her.

"All I'm trying to say is that Black people are people. Black issues are human issues. Terrorism doesn't have acceptable levels."

Winston hugs Lori while she cries. He kisses her on the forehead.

Winston smiles at her and jokingly inquires, "Now...how about a blow job?"

Lori looks back at him with a straight face, and they both laugh.

"Let's try to get some sleep," Winston says. "We need to leave before dawn breaks."

He squints at the alarm clock.

"Damn. This thing is brighter than daylight."

Opening the nightstand drawer, he discovers an envelope and an old map. He retrieves both items and uses the envelope to shield the intrusive glow of the digital clock.

Walking over to his bag, he retrieves a black hoodie and uses it to cover the small window, plunging the room into complete darkness. He and Lori settle in and Lori goes straight to sleep. Winston closes his eyes but can't; he's still wired from everything that happened earlier.

He stays up and decides to watch some television.

It's still dark in the room but his eyes adjust just enough to make out the location of the furniture.

He inspects the nightstand, searching for a TV remote near where his phone is charging. Winston, sucking his teeth, whispers, "No remote." He climbs out of bed and inspects the area around the TV. He remarks, "No remote here either."

Returning to the bed, he reaches over to turn on the light but stops as he remembers that Lori is asleep. He mutters, "Where's that flashlight?" He reaches for his bag and quietly rummages through it. His eyebrows furrow in confusion as he feels something hard and rectangular in his hand. He pulls it from the bag; it's a remote. He whispers, "How did this get in here?"

He points the remote in the direction of the TV and presses the power button, and miraculously it turns on.

With a quiet sense of triumph, he remarks, "Thank goodness, finally a win!"

The national anthem begins to play as the American flag flutters in the wind. He positions himself quietly and starts pressing buttons to change the channel, but static and snowflakes appear with each click.

He starts to feel frustrated. Even defeated. "Where's Netflix when you need it? This place is probably still on dial-up internet."

He clicks one more time and much to his surprise "The Dell Ferrell Show" comes on. Ferrell is in the middle of an interview.

Winston remarks, "Not this clown again."

An audience member stands in front of a vintage microphone before a hushed audience. He asked, "What y'all got against plantations? I see them more as tourist attractions than anything else."

The audience claps, chatters, and whistles loudly.

Dell Ferrell interrupts, "Hold on, hold on. I'm sure our guest Mr. Mannings has nothing against our beautiful, historic Southern sites."

The camera pans over to his seated guest, whom Dell refers to as "Cuz Mannings." He is a stern-looking, middle-aged Afro-Latino man wearing a colorful dashiki and black slacks; calmly sitting across from Dell.

Cuz responds to the audience member's question. Smooth, and his tone is even with not even a hint of aggression. He leaves that for his words.

"Historic sites are not Disneyland. U.S. history is not fantasy or folklore, and plantations are inherently uncomfortable places for Black people. If tourists dared to ask deeper and more nuanced questions, I promise that they will receive answers that challenge

America's reimagined history. White folks love the word "Plantation" because it evokes opulent estates, green grass, and weeping willow trees."

He pauses and directs his intense gaze to Dell.

"However, if you're Black, all you see is an amusement park for rape, murder, torture, and loss."

Dell is spent and leans back. The audience gasps.

Winston's face breaks into a wide grin as he peers down at Lori, who is peacefully sleeping beside him. He extends his hand to wake her and expose the show to her. However, just as he does, the TV crackles and the screen fills with snowflake static, abruptly interrupting the show.

Winston stops his attempt to wake Lori and starts frantically pressing the remote control in his hand, trying to get back to the Dell Ferrell Show. Sadly, with a press of a button, the TV screen goes dark, shutting off completely.

Lori wakes up, yawning, and asks, "Did you set the alarm?"

He answers, careful to keep any frustration out of his voice. "Thanks for reminding me. I'll do it now."

He reluctantly sets the remote down, picks up his cell phone, and sets the alarm for 3:45 a.m. Lori rolls over and goes back to sleep.

They are sound asleep when the cell phone alarm suddenly blares, intermittently lighting up the darkened room. Winston wakes up abruptly and swipes at the phone, silencing the alarm.

He rolls over to rouse Lori awake.

With a scratchy voice, she complains, "It's so early. Can't we just stay another day?"

Winston replies as he pulls a T-shirt over his head, "Absolutely not. It's go time, so get dressed."

Lori moans as she groggily begins to dress herself. Winston heads to the bathroom and closes the door behind him.

When Winston returns, his mood has improved enough to attempt a joke.

"Yeah, It's definitely a shit show in there, but no moving wallpaper to keep me entertained!"

Still tired, Lori just asks a question. "How much time do we have?"

Winston glances at his cell phone. "About 20 minutes or so."

He heads over to the window, removes his black hoodie, and puts it on.

Lori slowly makes her way into the bathroom while Winston packs everything up. He stares at the remote control before shaking his head and shrugging. He places the remote back into his bag and waits for Lori near the door.

She emerges from the bathroom fully dressed, slipping on her shoes as she moves.

Winston checks the time on his cell phone; it displays 4:33 a.m.

His adrenaline pumps, while the words of the bellboy ring in his head.

"Ready?" He asks.

They clasp each other's hands.

Lori nods her head and says, "Ready!"

The Railroad Tracks

Suited men funnel into the prestigious library of the grand Sinclair Estate. There, the descendants of the Sinclair family gather to discuss plans for their most valuable commodities. They all understand that their inherited project, initiated by their fathers and their fathers' fathers, always comes first. A legacy project that is both ambitious and notorious.

Robert Sinclair, the patriarch of the family, a man with silver hair and dazzling green eyes, stood before an imposing wooden table covered in maps, old leather-bound journals, and a faded blueprint of a railroad that connects the South to the North. The Sinclair family had always been known for their vast wealth and their ability to keep their secrets hidden.

"Gentlemen," Robert began, his voice tinged with a sense of solemnity, "You know what we are about to discuss. It is part of our inheritance and what keeps our family connected to wealth. The railroad is not just about connecting two regions; it is about protecting our legacy and securing our future."

The men exchanged glances, fully aware of their lineage and expectations. Their fathers had entrusted them with its continuation.

As the room filled with whispered discussions, Robert continued.

"Our predecessors had their reasons for constructing this railroad, and those reasons benefit us to this day. We have inherited not only their ambitions but also their secrets."

Their plan involved not only the acquisition of discreet parcels of land but also the construction of a labyrinthine network of chambers that would lie beneath the tracks. To maintain their dealings, they employed a network of loyal agents and legal experts who worked tirelessly to acquire the land without drawing undue attention. The properties were bought under various aliases, and their true purpose remained hidden from the prying eyes of regulators and curious onlookers.

They were not the only ones with a vested interest in the secrets buried beneath the tracks. Governors, heads of state, and even the President had heavy stakes in the Railroad. However, times were changing, and the risk of exposure had become real. Members from their own association had threatened to expose their dark family history and unravel their carefully guarded secrets. They meet today to secure their legacy and preserve the railroad that had bound their family together for centuries.

Within that same week, in an Atlanta motel room, a nude White man with piercing blue eyes, and scruffy curly brown hair is crouched in the corner on the floor. He moans in pain with his arm outstretched and views the back of his hands and the skin on his arms. His hand begins to tremble, he frantically searches his mind for answers.

He continues to sob a mournful symphony echoing through the otherwise still air. On the bed, a jumble mess of clothing and several bobble-headed figurines lie strewn, alongside a lone lanyard adorned with the insignia of the Southern Republic, bearing the identification of one Lewis, Lilbert - Staff Reporter for The Southern Republic.

A man enters from the other room, sitting on the edge of the bed, his image darkened by the closed curtains. His voice is deep and gruff as he explains, “You can’t win, and you can’t get out of the game." Lilbert, choking back tears, asks, "What did you do to me?" The stranger replies, "Me? Nothing. I'm just here to watch."

Days after Lilbert went missing, his sister, Corrine, had been searching for him as well. After numerous unanswered phone calls and text messages, she decided to visit his house. Corrine stepped out of her car in front of Lilbert's small bungalow-style home. She pans her eyes up and down on his well-manicured block and begins to move towards the front door.

As she approaches the front door, she notices that it is slightly ajar. Corrine peeks inside and gently pushes the door open further. Stepping inside, her eyes need a moment to adjust to the partially dim interior. All the blinds are closed, and the only light filtering through is the thin slivers between each blade of the blinds.

Cautiously, Corrine walks through the house, scoping out her surroundings, and calls out, "Lilbert… Are you home? I've been trying to reach you for two days."

She tiptoes through the living room and dining area, the hardwood floors protesting with every step as they emit faint creaks beneath her weight. In the dimly lit dining room, an empty table and chair come into view, and a small fan whirs on the table.

Corrine fixates on the chair, noticing a thin layer of brown dust settled upon it. She draws nearer, her curiosity piqued, and as she inches closer, she hears a faint crunching sensation under her shoes. Looking down she sees dark, crispy flakes peppered around the floor near the chair.

She proceeded cautiously, galvanizing herself with humor. Nevertheless, she whispered. "You need a maid, baby brother?"

As she explores the small house, she notices that all of Lilbert's belongings are still in place. Her footsteps lead her toward the bedroom, a hopeful notion crossing her mind that he might be asleep.

Upon entering the room, she notices that the curtains are drawn closed, allowing only a sliver of light to penetrate. Corrine reaches for the light switch, but the lights don't turn on. After her eyes adjust to the dimness, she can make out a dark figure lying on the bed. Feeling a sense of relief, she walks past the bed and makes her way over to open the curtains.

As she pulls back the curtains, the room is flooded with light. To her horror, the shadowy figure on the bed is not Lilbert at all; it's a grotesque, gooey stain in the shape of Lilbert, filled with the same crispy brown flakes she found in the dining room.

Corrine startles, jumps backward in shock, and rushes out of the house in a panic. In her frantic exit, she stumbles down the front stairs and rolls to the side of her car. After gathering her wits, she climbs into her car and swiftly dials a number, anxiously saying, "Yes, Police? I need to report a missing person."

CHAPTER SEVEN

In their room at Bee-Bee's B&B, Winston slowly opens the door. They walk out, and the door closes with a resonant thud. The bang of the door reverberates through the floor, causing the envelope covering the digital clock to fall away. Where the illuminated time on the clock reads 3:33 a.m.

Winston tries to guide Lori as quietly as he can through the darkened hallway. The corridor is dimly lit, with exposed pipes dripping. As they advance through the corridor, a sudden whizz overhead catches their attention. They look up and see more exposed pipes, oozing a mysterious liquid.

This prompts them to look down, discovering a wet and sticky carpet that clings to the soles of their shoes. Winston decides to use the light on his phone to guide them to the winding staircase. As they continue walking, they hear unnerving moans in the distance.

In the quiet shadows of the dimly lit hallway, Lori's voice emerges in a soft whisper, barely more than a breath, "Did you hear that?" Winston, his voice equally subdued, replies, "Unfortunately, yes."

They press on, each step measured, their hands firmly clutching their luggage, until they reach the entrance to the stairway. There, a solitary, flickering fluorescent light casts eerie shadows upon the scene. As they approach, the haunting moans draw nearer, their resonance growing louder in the stillness. Lori, her empathy evident, comments, “Somebody needs help.”

With frustration seeping through his words, his answer is sharper than he intends. “Shit, Lori, WE need help! We’ve got to get out of here. We’re on the clock.”

He steals a glance at Lori, her eyes silently pleading for a different course of action. Reluctantly, he sighs and utters, “Dammit, woman!”

He releases Lori’s hand, places one bag over his shoulder, and sets the other bags down. Lori follows suit. Winston proceeds past their intended stairwell and continues farther down the hall. In the hallway, Winston could discern several closed doorways, with the exception of one door slightly ajar. They move toward it cautiously. Winston leans in, poking his head through the opening.

A fluorescent tube light overhead flickers erratically. Winston, owl-eyed, gasps.

Lori attempts to peer over his shoulder.

A Black woman lies on a soiled mattress on the floor, a large lock of straight blonde hair hanging over her forehead. Various food and drink items are strewn across her waist, legs, and feet, with pomegranate seeds scattered across her midsection.

Her feet and calves are dark-skinned, while the skin on her thighs is mottled, gradually transitioning to a pale white color. As Winston pans upward, he notices that her thighs, torso, and forearms are white as well.

However, her hands, neck, and face are as dark as her legs. The flickering light reflects off of her showing that she is covered in a wet viscous substance. She wails while the sticky substance oozes from her mouth, and squirts from under her dress.

Winston pushes Lori back as he enters the room. Lori peeks in. He whispers angrily,

“Lori, I mean it. Stay there!”

Allowing curiosity to overcome her, Lori asks, “What’s wrong with her?”

The woman sobs and tries to move, saying, “It hurts... it hurts.”

Winston hesitates but moves slightly forward. He looks around the room before he addresses the woman.

“Jesus, take the wheel. What did they do to you?”

The woman cries but manages to answer. “They’re forcing me to eat it. I didn’t want to do it.”

“Eat what... You know what.” He begins to shake his head in disbelief and continues, “Nope…Nope. It doesn’t even matter.” He begins to backpedal.

Lori’s grip tightened on Winston’s back repeatedly chanting, “Oh My God!” He could feel a panic attack coming on; he was becoming lightheaded and dizzy.

He stops once more to stare at the woman. “Look, lady, I’m sorry, but—”

The woman desperately reached out to Winston. Strings of viscous fluid dangled and dripped from her hands and arms. She begins to wiggle, attempting to free herself from the grip of the honey-like fluid. The struggle must have agitated her system and she started to violently vomit up the fluid.

Winston grabs Lori’s hand, and they bolt down the darkened hall. As they proceed from that point, the hallway has several open doors on either side. They feel the ground bounce under their feet. Stopping in their tracks, they press themselves against the wall in the darkness. With only a thin veil of shadows to conceal them, the pair must remain as quiet as possible to evade discovery.

Bertha Bellows comes into view, marching toward the door leading to where the woman remains stuck to the floor, still begging for help.

Bertha leans in. “Who you talking to, Denise? Ain’t nobody gonna help you. You’ve already eaten the food. You Blacks don’t never turn down a free drink or meal. Look at cha’ now, full of my sap.”

Bertha creeps into the room and disrobes from her top to her waist. Her otherwise white bra has brown stains peppered throughout and can barely contain her heaving bosom.

Denise begs. “No, not again…No.”

Bertha lets out a maniacal laugh as she peels back a brassiere cup revealing that her breasts are long, lumpy, and misshapen.

A symphony of cracks, smacks, and pops sound through the air.

Her nipples look like hardened nozzles. They leak that same brown, thick honey-like fluid that’s all over the floor. She squats down and forcibly shoves her nipple into Denise’s mouth. Denise gurgles and chokes but Bertha just strokes Denise’s hair while she feeds her.

“It’s OK…You’re almost there.”

Winston and Lori can hear the horror broadcasting from down the hall. Winston motions to Lori to enter another nearby room. The closest room to their position is pitch black. He looks at Lori and shrugs his shoulders, indicating their limited options. She reluctantly nods in agreement.

Once inside the room, they realize it’s even darker than the sacred spot they had in the hallway.

Lori whispers, "I can't carry these bags anymore," and gently sets them on the floor. They stand motionless, listening for Bertha to leave. Suddenly, the sounds of soft sloshing echo in the space. Winston presses his lips to Lori's ear and says, "There's an echo… this place must be enormous."

The pair press themselves against the wall as they navigate the space, and indistinct gurgles begin to bounce off the ceiling.

Lori asks, "What's that noise and that repugnant smell?"

Winston tries to joke.

"I. Don't. Know. This is my first time in Hell, too!"

He pulls out his phone, turns on the flashlight, and shines the light downward around the room. A horde of naked Black people with large white spots all over their bodies are in a huge pool filled to the top with the sticky brown fluid. Some are trapped below, some are partially submerged, and some are bobbing face down in the fluid. All of them are twitching and glitching. The air is thick with black dust.

Lori lets out a loud scream.

The floor creaks behind them, and a black hand extends out to cover Lori's mouth.

Winston quickly turns around and shines his flashlight in that direction. It's the bellhop, squinting at them, he turns his head to avoid the light in his eyes.

With a low voice, Winston asks, "What is this place? What are y'all doing to these people?"

The bellhop beckons them both to move softly backward with him. He checks the hall, and they all quietly tiptoe to another door that leads them to a massively ornate stairwell.

The stairwell is a sight to behold. Its white marble steps bear delicate wisps of black veins, adding an elegant touch. The banisters, resembling ornate crown molding, feature a splendid metallic gold overlay. Each step's width appears generous enough to accommodate an entire choir. The brilliance of the lighting is so intense that it gives the impression of a dedicated spotlight shining upon it.

Winston and Lori look around, covering their eyes until they adjust to the light and the blinding brilliance of the craftsmanship of the staircase.

However, the bellhop is angry. He scolds them saying, "Why are you roaming around? I told you to stay in your room until 4:33!"

Confused, Lori stutters, "We... We did."

The bellhop looks at his watch and states, "It's just now 4:22."

Winston frantically looks at his cell phone, regretfully replying, "My phone is still on Eastern. Fuck! Fuck! Fuck!"

The bellhop begins to shake his head and warns them.

"If they catch you out here, they're going to force-feed you that shit. The doors are on a timer. They're locked until 4:33 a.m. You can't go back to your room, and you can't stay here. Believe me when I tell you, you don't want that 'Honey'."

Lori quickly asks, "What's wrong with the Honey?"

He turns to Lori staunchly, even as his voice softens.

"Young lady, it's not... Honey. That's just what they call it because it's thick, brown, and sticky. There's no description for what it tastes like. Miss Bellows and her kinfolk got a condition that makes them drip this nasty brown sap. Once you've eaten in this place, the sap finishes you off...for good. This place is a portal to Hell!"

Winston frowns in recognition. "Whew…I saw it! Now I can't unsee it."

The bellhop taps his temple with his index finger.

"It messes with your mind. I mean... I know I'm Black and I don't belong here. But when that sap gets up in you, you don't want to leave."

He walks a couple of feet. "It doesn't make sense, 'cause they don't give you anything here. But that sap makes you happy with nothing!"

His mannerism suddenly changes. He glances up to the top of the staircase and stares as he strokes his chin.

"They've been taking us for years. The ones they can't turn, they go under the tracks."

The bellhop continues without answering Winston. "Ohhh... And you gotta be dark."

Lori is disgusted when she asks, "Dark?"

The Bellhop looks to Lori and then to Winston, asking, "Did you see that man earlier...the one with those blue fingernails? They don't want him. Noooo, he's too light. You are, too, Miss Lady. Not enough melanin to siphon off."

He raises his index finger as if touching something only he can see.

He chuckles. "But he ain't getting away though. They got other plans for him. But the darkies... oh, they love us. We're that coal that keeps the oven burning around here. That sap loosens our melanin…"

Shaking his head from side to side in dismay, Winston mutters under his breath. "Them damn 'Pretty Tonys'... they always had it easy."

The bellhop gives Winston an annoyed look and chastises him.

"This isn't a joke. It's something terrible to see and even worse to feel."

He stands defiant while he lectures Winston.

"Imagine your blackness floating off into the air like dust." He billows his hand in the air as he speaks. "These Bellows Bees, they gather it like pollen."

The bellhop's gaze shifts from the top of the stairwell to Winston and back again.

Then, he refocuses on their conversation.

"But never mind all that. I'm going to get you out of here."

With heartfelt gratitude, Winston says, "Sir, I don't know who you are or what's going on, but thank you."

He extends his hand, and the bellhop shakes it.

Meanwhile, Lori wanders closer to the steps of the stairwell, her mind flitting in and out of thoughts while Winston and the bellhop speak; she is still preoccupied with the musical notes in the murals. Unconsciously, she began to hum the strange notes of the Fugues.

Winston is elated that the bellhop is there to help. He'd forgotten his manners for a moment, asking, "By the way, what's your name?"

Lori's humming becomes noticeably louder, and the expression on the bellhop's face turns sour. He begins to squeeze Winston's hand tightly.

The bellhop slowly turns and looks at Lori, suddenly blinking and glitching as if experiencing some type of mechanical malfunction. His head twitches from side to side, accompanied by short clicking sounds emanating from his lips.

In pain, Winston screeches as the bellhop's grip tightens.

"Agh... Ow!"

It is something about Lori humming the Fugue that seems to have triggered the bellhop.

The bellhop looks down and begins blinking profusely. His face freezes, but he continues to shake Winston's hand, staring at

Winston eye-to-eye. His body starts to jolt, and then the bellhop abruptly opens his eyes and mouth big and wide, and he screams loudly.

"They're here! This Nigga trying to leave! I got 'em... They're here!"

Winston panics and attempts to pull his hand away. His heart races, and his vision warps. The bellhop's screaming continues. "They're in the main stairwell! They're here!"

Lori bolts up the stairs and leaves Winston without a second thought. She takes a deep breath and returns to help but stops halfway. She cries, muffling her sobs by putting her hand over her mouth. Winston punches the bellhop, and brown ooze shoots from his nose and mouth, forcing him to let go.

Winston dashes up the stairs to meet Lori, and together they sprint to the main floor. As they reach the landing, catching their breath, they realize that the stairwell has led them to within a mere twenty feet of the front door. Lori's excitement bubbles up, and she cheers as they make a beeline for the front door, pushing with all her might. However, to their dismay, the door doesn't budge. In the distance, the shuffling footsteps of a large, ominous group echo down the corridor.

Winston swiftly turns to face the approaching shadows, their heavy footsteps resonating alongside a strange, unsettling buzzing noise.

He picks up a chair and hurls it at the door. The chair shatters, but the door remains intact. Lori drags a planter over. When she moves it, she spots a turquoise fingernail on the floor. She continues to drag the planter, struggling as she barely lifts it and gently bumps it against the glass. It doesn't break.

Lori shouts, "What time is it?"

Winston kicks and pushes at the door.

Bertha, accompanied by several of her hulking and deformed kinfolk, arrives in the lobby. She grins at the pair, then puts her fingers in her mouth and emits a high-pitched whistle, prompting her kinfolk to advance.

In a panic, Winston yells, “Oh shit!”

Meanwhile, a terrified Lori screams, “WINSTON!”

The lock’s timer trills, and then the lock itself turns, and pops. The doors unlock, and they push them open. Winston and Lori rush outside.

Winston and Lori finally make it to the parking lot, but the pursuing mob is relentless.

In a swift motion, Winston retrieves his car key while on the move. He deactivates the car alarm with a chirp, unlocking the doors and they waste no time diving into the vehicle.

The angry, dripping, and sticky mob comes to a stop, visibly agitated, growling, barking, and beating their chests as the couple rolls away.

As they speed past the woods at the end of the parking lot, a black rabbit suddenly hops into view. Winston stares at the rabbit as they speed down the road. The rabbit remains seated, innocently blinking at Winston, as if bidding him a silent goodbye.

Bertha stands at the top of the stairs with a menacing demeanor. She, too, spots the black rabbit sitting in the parking lot. She motions to one of the men to capture the rabbit. He walks over to the rabbit and picks it up. Then he holds the squirming rabbit to his mouth and drips sap onto its face.

He turns to face the car, which is nearly out of view, and smiles, revealing dagger-like, rotting teeth. Some of the fur on the rabbit begins to fade from black to white. Then, Bertha whistles a high-pitched tone, and the disfigured mob swiftly turns, reentering the B&B with the rabbit in hand.

CHAPTER EIGHT

It's early morning now. Despite that, Winston drives until he feels they are miles away from the nightmare. He scans his surroundings and eases the car into a dense thicket of woods. A train rumbles along a nearby track and sounds its horn into the wilderness. Still breathing heavily, they continue to check if anyone is following them.

Lori is the first to break the silence.

"We have to get out of here and call the police on these people!"

Winston looks at Lori incredulously. "I think this goes beyond the police."

She looks at him with concern. "Well, if you won't call the police, then we need to find an airport or something. This trip isn't worth risking our lives."

He callously replies, "I know it's fucked up, and believe me, I'm terrified as shit. But as a Black man with missing family members and a journalist, I owe it to the world to reveal what's going on. At the very least, share what might have happened to thousands of people."

Lori's eyes fill with tears, and she angrily shouts. "Fuck the world! You owe me."

She pointed a stiff finger at herself, screeching, "It's your job to protect me!"

Exhausted, Winston reclines his seat.

"I am…I will! Just think about it, it's 2015. If this stuff is happening to us right now, then imagine what they went through back then? Imagine having to endure these situations on foot, with babies in tow? They couldn't just bail and hop on Delta!"

Lori wipes her tears, turns her head, and stares out of the window.

Winston continues his explanation. "When we first got together, you said that you were all in. Well, this is what 'all in' looks like!"

Lori looks at him with surprise. She begins to yell. "We were having sex, Winston! Of course, I said I was all in!"

Winston smiles, instantly changing the mood. "Look, it's you and me against the world. Right…right?" He takes her hand in his. "We can do this. It's just a few more states to go. We're almost there."

Lori somberly nods in agreement. Just then, her stomach growls and reverberates throughout the car. They both look down at her stomach.

Then Winston jokingly speaks in the direction of her stomach, "Thanks for the reminder! I Googled a down-home barbecue place, and it's not far. Let's grab something to eat. I think things will look different then. Okay?"

Lori's eyes light up. "Barbecue? Oh my God, yes!"

Winston turns the key in the ignition, and with a roar of the engine, they drive off.

They drive up a gravel road and park in front of "Papa Bear's Bar-b-Cue," a small, old cabin-style shack nestled in a clearing within the woods.

Lori leans forward in her seat as the car approaches. "The food is going to be great; look at those massive meat smokers on the side over there."

Winston parks swiftly, and they eagerly exit the car. As they walk arm in arm up the creaky wooden stairs, smoke billows out of the smokers. Lori grins, taking several deep breaths, and says, "Do you smell that? They really know how to cook real barbecue!"

Winston chuckles affectionately. "What do you know about some authentic barbecue? Black folks have the 'Cue' on lock."

He smiles at Lori and pulls her closer. They reach the weather-beaten door, and he grasps the handle, ushering Lori in first. As soon as they step over the threshold, a bell chimes.

Upon entering, they instantly feel comfortable with the aesthetics of the place. Papa Bear's Bar-b-Cue looks more like an old down-home country store than a barbecue joint.

"I love it! It's like Cracker Barrel," Lori says.

Winston jests under his breath. "Yeah... only without whip-wielding racists."

Lori gives him a disappointed look. "Shhh… Stop it, they'll hear you!"

They were the only two customers in the quaint establishment. As they stroll through the cozy space, they notice several eat-in tables. Behind the counter, they see a well-equipped cooking area with a time-tested grill.

Out of the blue, whacking sounds lead their eyes further into the open kitchen area, where an old, haggard White lady vigorously chops grilled meats with a gleaming cleaver. A loud cough gives way to one additional occupant, a country bumpkin-looking fellow who is leaning against the wall, wearing a pair of "Oshkosh B'gosh" overalls and chewing on a long piece of hay straw.

The leaner makes his presence known again by loudly cackling, "Look Ma, we got some company!"

The woman behind the counter never turns around to acknowledge her customers. She belts out, "What are you telling me for, Skipper? Take their damn order!"

She continues to chop at whatever is on the table, while Winston and Lori try to see what poor creature she was decimating from a distance. But she was standing in such a way that they could never see around her to make it out.

Skipper casually saunters around the corner and positions himself beside the register, holding a pen and notepad. His accent is stereotypical for the backwoods of Alabama, however, he seems to have a signature twist. Asking "What'll it be fo' ya'll there nah?"

Winston answers a question with a question. "You got a menu?"

Ma quickly shouts, "No menu. We only got one thing... grilled meat."

Lori happily bounces up to the counter, saying, "Sounds good. We'll take two orders of grilled meat and a couple ah' cokes."

Ma finally turns around with a massive machete-type cleaver in her hand. Her face is unfriendly and hardened. It looks like years of smoked meat and menthols have taken their toll. She had on an odd dusty, gray wig that sat too far down on her forehead.

Winston recoils at her appearance and something else he can't quite put his finger on.

Ma laughs. "Y'all must be new around these parts."

She points the cleaver at Skipper and waves it in his direction. "This is what they call...what's that word, Skipper?"

He begins to laugh hysterically and answers "Irun-neck, Ma!"

Winston shoots a strange look over at Lori and looks back at the mother and son duo comically. He informs them, "I think the word you're looking for is ironic."

While they jokingly exchange words, Lori wanders over to a shelf that has handmade snack bags with a clear plastic window revealing the contents inside. The bag's label reads "Homemade Jerky."

She picks it up and inspects it. "Now, this looks good, and it'll stay fresh while we're on the road. I love dried meats!"

She attempts to open the bag. Winston quickly walks over, takes the bag from her, and puts it back on the shelf. "Save your appetite for the real meal." He leans over closely to Lori and warns her. "Besides, it looks a little roadkill-ish."

Lori slightly backs away and gives a look of disgust.

Ma walks to the counter, revealing smears of brownish-green oil all over her hands and forearms. Small chunks of translucent fat and pinkish meats are dotted on her hands and forearms. Ma repeats the order. "Two large grilled meats and two cokes."

Lori appears concerned after looking at what Ma is covered in. "Is this pork or beef?"

Ma and Skipper look at each other and laugh out loud.

Ma replies, "It's gon' be the best pig you done ever ate! Since y'all is new, first meal's on us!"

Winston breaks into the conversation. "Wow, thanks! Dinner's on us next time!"

Skipper belts out, "Oh…it will be!"

Winston curiously sniffs the air. "This barbecue really smells different," he says.

Skipper giggles and starts to hum the tune "Dueling Banjos" from the movie "Deliverance." Winston scowls at Skipper.

Ma jumps in. "Shut your trap, Skipper. Don't make me say it again!"

She directs her attention to Winston. "Sorry 'bout that folks. He's a fuckin' idiot sometimes, but he means well." Skipper lowers his head and meanders off to the side.

Winston mumbles under his breath. "Yeah, cut it out, Skipper...before I kick your ass."

Ma clears her throat. "That's the marinade I use. Sometimes the meat can be a little tough and chewy. My marinade makes it melt in your mouth like butter."

She looks at Lori. "What kinda sauce you want on that?"

Lori brightens. "If you have spicy, I'll take that."

Winston speaks out in agreement. "Me too." Ma ladles on the sauce, boxes up the meat, and hands Lori the bag with their food in it.

Winston jingles, "Thank you! It's been real!"

As they walk out, Lori reminds Winston, "Babe…they forgot our Cokes." They stop and turn to go back to the counter.

Winston says, "What about the Cokes?"

Ma has stepped away from the chopping table, and the pair has a clear view of what is there. A charred severed arm with the hand attached dangling from a meat hook. It had bits of brown skin and oily pink meat showing. All the nails are turquoise blue with the exception of the missing nail on the index finger.

Lori is horrified! Winston's mind rewinds to the last thing that the bellhop told them and to the last person he saw with blue nails. Skipper smiles menacingly at Winston, and Lori instantly drops the packaged food on the floor.

Skipper shouts. “They know, Ma, they know!”

Thunderous footsteps can be heard along with doors opening and closing. Winston’s eyes are trained on Skipper, while Lori is watching for Ma. Muffled noises emanate from the rear of the store.

Ma has yet to be seen, but she is yelling orders to her son. “Get ‘em, Skipper. I’m calling the boys now. Don’t let ‘em leave! I wanna get that yellow girl on the grill!”

Lori panics after hearing Ma’s demands. Skipper advances on Winston. Lori tries to help fend him off, but Skipper proves to be craftier than he looks. As the men fight, they knock over racks and shelves filled with food. While they fight, Winston drops his phone, and it lands on the floor.

Lori yells. “Stop…why are you doing this?”

While they fight, Winston’s phone rings. Despite trying not to get killed, he can’t help but glance over at it. The name on the screen read ‘Lilbert Lewis.’ While distracted and twisted in an unfortunate position, Skipper rolls onto Winston’s left foot and twists his ankle.

Winston writhes in pain and screams. “Ah, shit...my ankle.”

Lori hops around, circling the men as they fight, yelling, “Tell me what to do, baby!”

While on the floor tussling with Skipper, Winston looks up and sees a painting on the ceiling that resembles the paintings from the hotels. The painting has White people with black hands on a plantation doing chores. There is one enslaved woman whistling a long tune. Music notes stretching out far. Train tracks lead to their house like a walkway. Now Ma is approaching with a machete in her hand and two ropes knotted as nooses in the other.

Lori panics, grabs an iron fire poker that was for sale, and cracks Skipper over the head. She helps Winston up from the floor, and Winston quickly says, “Look up… Look up!”

Confused, Lori glances overhead and sees the mural. Ma advances swiftly, swinging the machete. Lori clumsily uses the fire poker to block the blade. The machete falls out of Ma's hand and hits the floor.

Lori swings the poker and it hooks Ma in the eye. Lori tries to pull it out but it's caught. Lori screams, "Oh God!"

Ma's head is dragged from side to side, so much so that her wig falls off revealing several random tattoos. One of the larger ones reads, "1776". Ma squeals and hits the ground. Mother and son wail on the floor, scraping to get up.

Lori goes to Winston and tries to lift him but takes a moment before she does to look at the mural on the ceiling one more time. Lori hums and cries erratically, "He-ha-um-ha-ah-oh-da-do-ra."

Winston yells. "Lori, what the hell are you doing? Let's go!"

Lori groans and takes Winston's hand, lifting him up, and they hightail it out of the restaurant. Once outside, they hear the engine of some kind of large vehicle.

Winston looks down the road to see a pickup truck full of angry guys barreling toward the restaurant. Lori cries out. "Get in, I'll drive." Winston tosses her his keys and they drive off in a hurry.

After successfully evading capture by another mob, they drive along quietly listening to "Top of the World" by The Carpenters on the radio. They're driving parallel to a train going in the same direction, only separated by a narrow forest area.

Winston nudges Lori. "My foot feels better. Pull over and let me drive."

She doesn't hesitate because she just learned to drive the year before and is still nervous about it. She pulls over and Winston gingerly walks to the driver's side and gets back on the road. Lori gets comfortable and digs in her bag for her musical notebook and begins to write.

As they make their way to the backwoods of Alabama, their stomachs growl ferociously. Their faces remain muted as they pass an off-ramp sign for a Mom and Pop restaurant. Looking at each other with the same sentiments, they continue and drive past the exit sign.

Winston pats his pockets. “Dammit, I lost my phone at Jeffrey Dahmer’s favorite Cue joint. Not to mention, I think Lilbert called me. Man…I really need to talk to him!”

Lori crosses her arms and looks over at Winston with a grimace.

“You’re worried about a co-worker after what we just went through? And we left nearly all of our bags at Bee-Bee’s. Now neither of us have phones and we’re clearly starving.”

“I know. I messed up. We’ll stop soon at a Walmart or something. We’ll find somewhere safe and catch our breath. I planned on us being in Chattanooga sometime today anyway. I hope we can be there in time for my doctor’s appointment. Let’s pull over and see exactly where we are—”

Lori interrupts him. “No need. There’s a sign right there. We’re in Tennessee. Congratulations. Now, I’m taking a nap to ward off my impending starvation.” She reclines and turns toward the window.

Winston reaches over and touches her arm. “Okay, but before you do all that… At the restaurant, what were you saying while you were looking at the ceiling?”

“The mural. It had musical notes, too, and they’re getting stranger and stranger. I don’t think that it’s just artistic license.”

“What do you think it’s about?”

Lori mumbles a non-answer. “I don’t know. I can’t think straight right now. Wake me when there’s food.”

She grabs a sweater, throws it over her face, and closes her eyes.

Hanna-May sat at a table and wrote music notes on a piece of parchment with a skinny stick that she used as a pen after she dipped it in a small glass bottle of black ink. Tufts of kinky black hair had escaped from her scarf that was tightly bound on her head. A kerosene lamp provided light, and a fireplace roared across from the table. She hummed the tune of the music notes she composed. Her voice changed inflections in tandem with the crackling fire. It sounded random and chaotic.

Behind her, the door creaked open, and a man's voice called out. He was out of breath. "Hanna-May, the group is outside hiding behind trees and in the bushes. We need the route. Is it finished?"

She turned around and revealed that her face was milky white with blue eyes, and she had a dark, heavily melanated neck, ears, and upper chest. She unrolled a large canvas with a painting on it. The scene depicted a Black woman surrounded by white people with fiery torches in the dark forest. Music notes flowed across the painting, fading into the forest scene.

She smiled. "Yes, Sir... it's done." She held up the painted canvas. Suddenly, a strange melody came from outside, startling Hanna-May's guest. She says, "Don't fret, it's just Ms. Elysses playing a Diddley Bow in the woods. She's letting me know it's safe to travel."

Ominous music from a Diddley bow continued to play.

Hanna-May continued to hold up the canvas, her eyes fixed on the intricate details of the painting. The Black woman in the center of the scene stood tall, surrounded by White figures whose faces bore expressions ranging from anger to curiosity. The fiery torches they held cast eerie, flickering shadows on the trees that backlit the forest like the sun preparing to rise. The music notes flowed across the painting, merging with the forest.

Her guest, a man with disheveled hair and dirt-streaked clothes, stared at the painting in awe. If anyone else saw this painting, they would not dare to guess the knowledge that it held. Hanna-May captured hatred perfectly and used it to guide her people to freedom and peace, not just with her notes but with her brush strokes as well.

She carefully rolled up the canvas, her fingers lingering on the edges as if she were saying a silent prayer to the artwork. She then turned to face her guest, her blue eyes meeting his with a mixture of determination and warmth.

"We have the route, Reemus," she said, addressing the man. "It's hidden within this painting, just like all the others."

Reemus nodded, his voice filled with gratitude. "Thank you, now we must go. We can be at the next marked home by morning."

Hanna-May smiled, her lips curved into a knowing grin. "Tell everyone not to come back here. My change is almost done. I won't be myself anymore. Promise me that these pieces of art will hang everywhere a Black foot may step. Prayerfully the song of the Diddley Bow will lead the way."

Reemus gently bowed his head to her and rushed out the door. Hanna-May carefully extinguished the kerosene lamp, leaving only the crackling fire. The ominous melody from the Diddley Bow outside continued to play, a haunting reminder of the challenges they all had to face on their respective journeys.

Closing the door, she sat stoically in front of a shattered mirror, anticipating the arrival of dawn. She understood that her moment of transformation was imminent, aware that the sap's alchemical magic would have her wake as a White woman by morning.

CHAPTER NINE

Winston and Lori arrive in the bustling city of Chattanooga, Tennessee.

He finds a parking spot on a busy street, blending in with the flow of life that surrounds them. Sitting there, he takes a moment to savor the normalcy of everyday living as people pass by. Lori is still sleeping, but he is anxious to show her that they are safe and amidst the living. He softly nudges her. "We made it!"

Lori yawns and stretches. She looks out of the window and sees people of all ages, including children. She excitedly gathers herself and exits the car, with Winston following suit.

Before she gets too excited, Winston lovingly holds both of her forearms.

"OK, here's the deal. My doctor's appointment is over there."

He motions across the street. "I'll meet you back here in about an hour. Stay put until I get back. I'll pick up a couple of temporary phones too."

Lori swoons. "Take your time, babe. I'm going to enjoy the food and relish the company of some BASIC crazy people."

Winston smiles and begins to walk away, then stops. “Can you save me a few ladyfingers to go with my coffee?”

“Really?” Lori’s eyes go wide.

He shrugs his shoulders and smiles at her. “Too soon?” He laughs.

Lori’s laugh isn’t as jovial. “Ha…Ha…Ha.”

They kiss and go their separate ways.

Neither of them notices, but a delivery truck passes behind them on the street. The side of the truck reads, “BEE-BEE’S HONEY,” with an accompanying slogan that reads, “The Honey With The Mother In It!” The truck parks on the side of a small grocery store down the street preparing to make a delivery.

Winston enters a well-lit doctor’s office bustling with people, the air carrying a distinct blend of lollipops and the sharp scent of Lysol. A multitasking receptionist immediately beckons him over, juggling a phone call and rapidly typing on a keyboard.

Approaching the desk, Winston observes as the receptionist discreetly mutes her phone conversation, reassuring him with a nod and a whisper. “I’ll be right with you, sir.”

Winston mouths his response. “No problem.”

She resumes her conversation, confirming an appointment with a caller. “Yes, ma’am. We’ll see you tomorrow at two. Uh-huh. Bye-bye.”

Transitioning her focus back to Winston, she apologizes. “Sorry about that. How may I assist you?”

“Yeah, I have an appointment to see Dr. Mancini. My name is Winston Gale.”

The receptionist promptly enters his name into the computer.

“I see you right here, Mr. Gale. Do you have insurance?”

Winston’s sigh is resigned. “Not anymore. I’ll be paying with a credit card.”

The receptionist updates the computer, calculating. "Alright. The initial visit, excluding prescriptions, will be $280.00, plus a 5% credit card transaction fee."

Winston sighs again. "Man…that's highway robbery."

She lowers her voice. "I know right. I promise you won't even be in there five minutes. I just changed my major to Pediatrics. They charge new moms even more."

Winston shakes his head and hands over his credit card.

She accepts it and begins speaking at a normal level. "Thank you, sir. Here's your receipt." She points down the hall."Dr. Mancini's office is in Room 108."

Winston raises an eyebrow, seeking clarification.

"Did you just say 108?"

The receptionist offers a reassuring smile. "Certainly...it's right over there. You're okay."

Winston hesitates briefly, then follows her indicated direction.

Upon reaching the examination room, Winston chooses a seat along the wall, positioning himself just outside the door. As he settles in, he absorbs the bustling atmosphere of ringing phones, the soft hum of elevator music, and the cheerful chatter and laughter of the people around him. Directly across from his seat is a magazine rack, brimming with periodicals and magazines.

Winston reaches for a magazine, flipping through its pages until an advertisement for a train cargo company snags his attention for some reason. The image depicts a powerful train roaring along the tracks in a picturesque countryside. The caption beneath the image proudly declares, "Tracking our way through America since 1828." After a moment, Winston continues to flip through the pages, then gently places the magazine back in its spot.

The doctor's examination room door is slightly ajar. Winston discreetly glances inside, spotting an older White gentleman in a crisp lab coat, standing across from a Black woman with her three- or four-month-old baby seated on the examination table. Their conversation is barely audible, with faint muttering reaching his ears. He quietly scoots closer to the door, keeping his back against the wall, and leans in closer to the door frame, trying to eavesdrop.

The baby coos as Dr. Mancini talks.

"However, I do want to start him on a low dose of Zencitravmasi. He's going to need it, particularly when he gets to be about ten or twelve years old. So it's best to start him off now."

The baby begins to cry.

"It can help with all the crying too."

The baby's mother chimes in. "Oh, before I forget. Can you refill my prescription too?"

"Sure thing." Dr. Mancini turns slightly and notices that the door is open, so he closes it.

Outside the door, Winston has a strange look on his face. He fishes the old medicine label out of his pocket and reads it. He pats his pockets, then remembers that he lost his phone.

Shortly afterward, the woman and her baby exit the doctor's office. Standing in the doorway, the doctor looks at his iPad and calls out. "Winston Gale!"

With his arm leaning against the door frame, Winston raises his hand in the air. "Yep…that's me!"

He stands and follows the doctor into the room.

"Nice to meet you, Winston. Have a seat." Winston sits on the examination table.

The Honey

This marks the sixth delivery of the day for Parker. As he carefully unloads the cases of honey from the truck, he finds himself greeted by the store's manager, Curtis Adams, on the busy loading dock. Curtis approached Parker with an unmistakable enthusiasm.

"I'm thrilled to see you here! We can hardly keep this product in stock."

Parker continues to methodically stack the honey cases on the dolly. "I've been delivering every Tuesday evening, just as always."

Curtis momentarily pauses, his gaze shifting to his phone's calendar.

"Oh, right... my mistake. Speaking of which, I tried calling the manufacturer in my confusion, but there was no answer, and no one returned my call. The former store manager left the books a mess. For the life of me, I can't find the manufacturer's information anywhere, just an email, a phone number, and a P.O. box.

Do you happen to have a contact person I could note down?"

Parker slows his pace, a perplexed expression crossing his face. "They're a small, family-run operation. They spend most of their time harvesting, but I'll inquire about a contact person for you the next time I pick up from them."

Curtis purses his lips and nods in agreement. As Parker pushes the cases into the store, Curtis accompanies him, continuing to ask questions with a touch of nervousness in his voice.

"I'd really like to arrange a tour of their facilities and take some photographs. I believe it could be a fantastic marketing opportunity to keep our sales strong. You folks are the reason we're in the black."

Parker maintains his steady pace with an effort to conceal the annoyance that had crept onto his face. He speaks with measured restraint. "Certainly, Mr. Adams, as soon as possible."

Curtis offers a congenial smile and wanders off to assist a waiting customer.

Once Parker finishes unloading and neatly arranging the jars on the store shelves, he wastes no time in heading back to his truck. Raising his cell phone to his ear, he dials a number. He's calm. "Let Bertha know it's time to set up shop."

He clicks his phone off, unbuttons his cuffs, and rolls up his sleeves, revealing a pair of stained and crusted bandages covering his forearms. He peels them off, unveiling deformity in his arms which are covered in a brown, sticky liquid. Parker puts the truck in gear, then drives down the street.

Back at Bee-Bee's, Harlow relays Parker's message directly to Bertha, who responds with a snide remark. "We should've stuck with the other guy. Everything was running smoothly until now."

Harlow is eager to be of help. "Is there anything I can assist with?"

Bertha holds up a sizable directory. "No, this is more than you can handle. We gotta get right for prying eyes. Just return to your desk; I've got this."

Harlow leaves the room, feeling somewhat sheepish.

Bertha dials a number on her phone and says, "Yeah, Jeb. It's time for a brick and mortar. Get all of the kinfolk together and make them presentable; well the ones that can be. We are about to go corporate. It's gonna be a big push!

The voice on the other end asks, "Should we reach out to the Presidential front runner?"

Bertha replies, "That needs not be your first call. He's down with the shits!" She lets out a loud round of laughter and hangs up.

Honey is the literal lifeline to the Bellows family. Bertha's ancestors had come a long way since their beginnings in London, England. In the mid-1500s, England began to experience strange occurrences in the area. Reports emerged of a set of sickly and misshapen babies born to the Bellows family. People had heard that they suffered from an unknown condition that caused the pores of their skin to weep a rancid, brown fluid.

Local doctors and scientists were summoned to the home of Bergen and Vanessa Bellows, only to return scratching their heads in dismay. The notes in their journals documented that the infants were covered in a foul type of resin that oozed from their skin. Additionally, the children refused to consume milk, whether from their mother or a cow.

Dr. Robert Wadewater heard about these peculiar events and brought along his African female servant, Attalah, to assess the babies' current condition. After conversing with the parents and inspecting the infants, he made a suggestion. Dr. Wadewater proposed allowing Attalah to nurse the babies, as he believed her milk contained a blend of human and other animal properties, a notion that Attalah knew to be false. She lowered her head in silence, unable to speak out.

She is reluctant to touch the babies but Wadewater has several men and waits for her to disrobe. With one baby suckling at each of her breasts, they ate ferociously until something unusual began to happen. Attalah's breasts began to turn as white as snow, and the infants' sticky, wet skin started to dry up and disintegrate into the air. The infants paused from drinking long enough to sniff the particles of dust wafting in the air. The remaining residue turned into thin, crackling material that could be easily peeled off.

Wadewater left Attalah there for several weeks. When he returned inquiring about his servant, the Bellows led him to a table where they and a female guest were having a meal.

Wadewater was impatient. "This is quite nice, but where is my servant girl?"

The young lady stood up. "Sir Wadewater, it is I, Attalah."

There stood a milky-White woman with blonde hair and emerald-green eyes. Shocked, he jumped back. "How?! How is this?!"

The Bellows couldn't explain how it happened, only what they observed.

Dr. Wadewater hurried to share the news with the King and Queen, and major news followed. There was talk of sending an envoy to explore a new world overseas, and on that boat were the entire Bellows family and Attalah.

Of course, Bertha Bellows is a descendant of Bergen and Vanessa, and her recent ancestors have found a way to utilize their hormonal sap in ways that not only benefit them personally but can also alter the landscape of North America.

Although Bertha Bellows does not have bees, she still makes and sells an ominous type of honey. They use a unique method for crafting and distributing honey to the masses. Imposing wooden containers resembling upright coffins, which serve as their nocturnal chambers, stand concealed within her property.

Each night, Bertha and her kinsfolk sleep within these strange structures, secreting a substance known scientifically as "Phlemanus." As the night unfolds, this simulated honey-like substance accumulates in a reservoir situated at the base of the boxes.

On a daily basis, they harvest this faux honey and prepare it for market consumption. To render it palatable for the everyday consumer, Bertha's ancestors devised the following recipe:

The recipe for "Phlemanus Honey" is listed as:

Phlemanus (Human Sap Excretions): 75%

Artificial Honey Flavoring: 15%

High Fructose Corn Syrup: 10%

As of today, there are many well-known franchise chicken restaurants that offer packets of delicious honey with their fried chicken and buttermilk biscuits. It might be a good idea to ask a question next time you go to one of those establishments, and before you accept a packet or 10. "Where is the honey from?"

Meanwhile, at Winston's medical appointment, Dr. Mancini asks a question of his own.

"It says that you're here for a refill of Zencitravmasi, 500mg?"

Winston is slightly embarrassed about the high dosage. "Yes, that's right."

The doctor begins to tap on his iPad. "Not a problem. I just need to look at your history and check your vitals. After that, we can get you on your way."

Winston raises his index finger in the air. "Before you do, a quick question?"

The doctor stops and takes a seat. "Sure. Go right ahead."

Winston finally asks the right question. "What is Zencitravmasi mainly used for? I mean, I know why I'm on it, but what else does it do?"

Dr. Mancini takes a deep breath before responding. "I've been prescribing it for years to combat veterans and POWs with extreme cases of PTSD. Even victims of attempted murder and kidnappings."

He lays the tablet down and proudly explains. "At its core, it manipulates the limbic system and the prefrontal cortex, which can regulate emotional behavior and dampen external fears or things perceived as dangers."

Smiling, he went on. "However, over time, we've found that it can treat all manners of conditions that need to be managed for the sake of society."

Winston offers a disapproving grimace and looks off for a moment before continuing his interview. "Prefrontal cortex, PTSD, and kidnapping victims? Man, what's really going on?"

Dr. Mancini quickly changes the subject. "Can we proceed with the exam? I have a busy schedule tonight."

Winston gives a disapproving tone. "Yeah, I guess so."

The doctor stands and places the stethoscope ear tips in his ears, then depresses the chest piece on Winston's back. Winston takes a deep breath.

As Winston leaves the doctor's office, he can't shake off the doctor's words. Right next door, by the cafe where Lori sat, stands Chattanooga RX, a pharmacy. Peering through the glass storefront window from the outside, Winston notices a line of people patiently waiting at the pharmacy counter. He goes in.

The pharmacy is not very big, and despite that, the line was nearly out the door with people waiting to be serviced. Winston casually stands with his prescription in hand while TV monitors are hanging from the ceiling overhead with an in-store commercial playing on a loop.

He glances up to see images of contented Black people appearing to collectively have a sense of happiness and well-being. In the midst of this, groups of Black men, women, and children stand in line near the pharmacy counter, where a White woman rapidly fills prescriptions as if she were on an assembly line.

Winston continues to scan the room where amongst the backdrop of customer conversations, serene music plays while the ads play overhead. A woman narrates. “With Zencitravmasi, it’s a better world on the other side.”

Then a male narrator speaks rapidly. “Medicines like Zencitravmasi can elevate risks for elderly individuals who have lost touch with reality. Patients of any age may experience heightened thoughts of self-harm and actions within the initial months of taking Zencitravmasi.”

As the commercial cycles back to its beginning, the serene music continues and the voiceovers fade into the background noise of the pharmacy.

Then the female narrator returns. “Life isn’t as bleak as it may seem. Sometimes, all it takes is a change of perspective.”

The pharmacist shouts. “Refill for Kimball. T. Kimball, please pick up your prescription.”

A tall middle-aged Black man walks up to the counter.

“Can you verify the name of your prescription, please?”

“Troy Kimball. Zencitravmasi, 250mg.”

The pharmacist is cheerful. “That’s correct. Thank you. Your co-pay is $20.00.” The customer runs his credit card, takes his purchase, and walks out of the store. Winston takes notice.

A young Black girl who appears to be in her late teens steps up to the window. Winston strains to hear her conversation with the pharmacist over the chatter and music, but she speaks in a low voice. Shortly after, she leaves the counter and takes a seat against the wall. The next customer approaches.

Next is an elderly Black woman holding a cane. The pharmacist types into her computer console. Winston scans the pharmacy and notices a clock on the wall. It reads 5:49 p.m. He then shifts his gaze back toward the counter.

The pharmacist speaks toward the seating area, slightly raising her voice. "Young lady... Young lady, you can come back up."

When the girl returns, the pharmacist advises her. "Here is your prescription. Your physician has prescribed a higher dose of Zencitravmasi. You can take them four times a day or as needed."

The pharmacist hands over the bag with her prescription, and the girl takes it and walks away.

Winston then looks down at his prescription, then back up at the line. He notices that several other Black people in the line are holding the same prescription in their hands.

Just then, the once serene music that played in the background seems to become distorted, with a dramatic musical note punctuating every time Winston focuses on a "Zencitravmasi" prescription in each customer's hand.

Winston panics and rushes out of the pharmacy before he can fill his prescription. He presses himself against the building's facade, doubling over. He's having an attack.

Gasping for air and feeling dizzy, his head spins. He can still hear a warped version of the music from inside the pharmacy. He looks at his prescription, balls it up, and throws it on the ground. He begins to walk away, but he quickly turns back around and picks up the wadded-up paper and goes back into the pharmacy.

CHAPTER TEN

Lori sits in a charming café adorned with a modern Steampunk industrial-themed decor. The floor features vibrant yellow-brick tiles that add a pop of color and warmth to the otherwise industrial surroundings. The walls are painted with blue skies and translucent clouds. The painted finish is adorned with vintage mechanical gears and cogs, creating an intriguing fusion of antique and futuristic elements. Large, hanging Edison bulbs cast a warm, ambient glow throughout the space, creating an inviting atmosphere.

However, the cafe's theme is in stark contrast to the music being piped in. Nipsey Hussle's 'All Get Right' fills the air via surround sound. Mounted on one wall, is a sizable TV monitor that plays a vintage 1974 episode of 'Match Game,' featuring the well-known actor of that era, Nipsey Russell, in an ironic twist. The TV remains muted, but closed captions are visible on the screen.

An older employee smiles and laughs as he looks up watching the monitor.

Across the room, Lori sits at a table, sipping coffee while dividing her attention between the customers engaged in lively conversations and her table, which is littered with half-eaten food.

She is so preoccupied that she doesn't see Winston sneaking up behind her. He startles her, and Lori jumps, swiftly turning around.

Yelling, "Oh my God…Winston!" she slaps his hand and he laughs.

Sitting down, he quickly picks up the menu and reviews it. Commenting, "Looks like you're enjoying yourself."

Lori leans back and rubs her tummy, grinning, "That I did!"

She waves over a waitress.

The waitress comes over wearing a black T-shirt with a logo that says "BackGrounds Coffee & Cafe" and a name tag that reads, "Ameerah."

She asks, "Are you ready for the check?"

Lori looks up, "Not yet. Can you bring my fiancé a—."

Winston interrupts, "A large coffee with cream, four raw sugars, and a shot of caramel."

The waitress quickly writes down his order. She states, "Got it!"

Winston continues, "Also, may I have a Chicken Sandwich with a Kale Salad?"

The waitress says, "Coming right up!" She spins off and walks away.

While they waited for his order, Lori asked, "How did your appointment go?" jokingly adding, "Did you re-up?"

Winston gives her a side-eye and says, "Oh…OK, I see. You got jokes. Please tell me you learned that from watching an old 'Boyz n the Hood' DVD or something and not from those hood rats you call friends."

The waitress returns with the food.

Smiling, Lori mocks, "Saved by the Kale."

Winston brushes off her jab and begins eating his food. Then he says, "By the way, I think you were right."

Lori asks, "Right about what?"

Winston takes another bite of his sandwich and chews.

He goes on, "The pills. I'm going to try a more holistic approach. I've been noticing some strange things since I ran out." He continues to eat, and Lori scoots closer to him.

Pompously, she replies, "I'm glad to hear that, babe!" Switching gears, she continues, "Did you see that nice hotel right down the street? We can get some real rest tonight and head out tomorrow."

Snapping, Winston screeches, "WOW! You glazed over that revelation rather quickly."

Lori shrugs her shoulders, snapping back, "I'm sorry. What was I supposed to say?"

Winston stops eating and loudly drops his fork.

Annoyed, he says, "I tell you that I'm no longer going to be taking a drug that I've been on since I can remember and that I have been noticing strange things since I've been off the medication. And your response is let's go to a fancy hotel?"

He takes another bite and continues, "Didn't we go over this already?"

Lori has a look of confusion all over her face as she says, "I just want to sleep in a safe place."

Winston pushes his food away and replies, "Lori, you can't have a Black fiancé, live on the Black side of town, have Black friends, and then want to disassociate yourself from Black issues."

Visibly upset, she charges, “Seriously? This, from a man with a Chinese girlfriend. I’m not disassociating myself from Blackness. I’m disassociating myself from dying.”

Winston waves his hand in the air to signal the waitress. She comes over and asks, “Would you like something else?”

He sharply replies, “Can you box this up? I’ll take the check.”

The waitress leaves the check, gathers the leftovers, and walks away.

He turns his attention back to Lori, saying, “Like I said before... I’m committed to this trip and whatever comes with it. Feel free to book yourself a flight. I’ll meet you in Chicago.”

Lori grabs her jacket and storms out.

Lori sits on the hood of the car, staring at Winston with a heated glare through the cafe’s glass window.

Winston pays the waitress and picks up the to-go bags. He walks out and stands in front of Lori.

Lori says, sadly, “I’ll finish the trip with you.”

He leans over and lifts her chin with his finger, staring affectionately into her eyes as he asks, “Are you certain?”

Pouting, Lori grabs the car door handle, but it doesn’t open. She mumbles out of embarrassment, “Just unlock the door.”

Winston depresses the key fob, and the car chirps, unlocking the door. Lori rushes to get in. Winston tosses the food in the back seat, gets in, and they pull off, heading to the next city on their list.

As they merge onto the highway, Lori inquires, “By the way, did you get the phones?”

Winston continues to drive, looking forward so that Lori cannot see the shame on his face. That because of his panic attack, he had forgotten to buy them.

He utters, “I looked, they were all out.”

They continue their trip in complete silence, each nursing their own wounds. Winston decides to break the ice, saying, "Babe, I'm glad you're doing this with me. Just think of the stories we can tell our grandchildren someday."

Lori remains silent, pretending to find interest in the passing scenery outside the window. They drive a bit farther, and finally, they are greeted by a breathtaking view as a highway sign announces their arrival: "Welcome to Kentucky."

Winston celebrates, "Look…we're in Kentucky. Indiana is up next, then on to Illinois." He cautions, "But, don't get too excited. Indiana is like the Texas of the Midwest. Big as hell and seems like it will never end."

Winston spots another highway sign, and it reads, "Vernon County Suites, Exit 21."

He quips, "Sounds like the perfect place, huh?"

He playfully pokes Lori with his elbow repeatedly.

Lori smiles, commenting, "I'm still mad, but it does sound nice."

Agreeing, he changes lanes saying, "Great…then we're on our way!"

Now that he's in a good mood, he turns on the radio and finds a station. "Love Ballad" by L.T.D starts to play, and Winston can't resist and begins to sing along with the music.

Lori, caught up in the mood as well, retrieves her notebook and starts reviewing it. She begins to hum the musical notes from her book and makes additional notes. Winston singing with all the grace of a feral cat doesn't hear Lori's rumblings.

She questions, "Oscarville?" She continues to write. She has a list of names in her notes. Memories of the writings and the musical notes on the hotel's wallpaper began to flash through her mind.

Winston was singing so loudly, and the car's music was blaring to such an extent that he couldn't hear Lori excitedly rattling a list off to him. She taps him on the arm as she continues to look at the book, trying to get his attention. She raises her voice, shouting, "Babe... Babe…!"

However, Winston continues to drive and sing, keeping his eyes fixed on the road ahead without responding.

Lori finally shouts at the top of her voice, "Winston!"

Thinking that she was alerting him to the exit, he quickly veers towards the off-ramp. As he does so, he passes by a blacked-out police car parked on the side of the road. Before they can take the exit, blue and red flashing lights come on, and a siren blares from the police cruiser now right behind them.

Winston pulls over, and suddenly, the weather takes a turn for the worse. The night sky is filled with rain, thunder, and lightning.

Winston squints to look through his side-view mirror, commenting, "Shit! I'm in trouble; he's White."

The officer lingers in his cruiser, talking on his walkie-talkie.

Lori comments, "Just chill. He pulled us over because you were kinda speeding. The police aren't out to get Black people!"

A sickly and panicked expression washes over his face. His heartbeat escalates as he reaches for his pill bottle and stares at the label. He becomes dizzy and starts to sweat profusely, seizing the wheel with a death grip.

After running Winston's plates, he begins to exit the car. He looks up at the falling rain, reaches into the backseat of his cruiser, and pulls out a white hoodie, putting it on. The hoodie is bright white except for reddish-brown stains that resemble dried blood, scattered on the sleeves.

He pulls the hoodie over his head and approaches the driver's side window of Winston's car. One hand is on his holstered gun, while the other shines a flashlight into Winston's car. He takes the flashlight and taps it on the driver's side window.

The officer smiles and shouts, "Roll your window down and turn off your engine... slowly." He unsnaps his holster.

Winston sits still for a moment, looking straight ahead. Then, he turns and looks up at the officer. The officer's hoodie is open, exposing his nameplate that reads "OFFICER NELIVEE."

With the flashlight shining in his eyes, the rain pouring down, and the officer's hood pulled down far over his face, Winston swears that he looks like a grim reaper.

The officer taps again. He says once more, muffled, "Roll your window down."

Winston shows his left hand to the officer and slowly moves to press the lever to open the window. Rain falls on Winston as he continues to look at the officer.

Lori leans across Winston, blatantly shouting over the rain, "How can we assist you, sir?"

Officer Nelivee bends down at the car's window; now he's within inches of Winston's face. Nelivee comments, "Unfortunately, little Miss Sunshine, you can't do nothin' but sit there and be quiet."

Lori rolls her eyes, crosses her arms, and leans back in her seat.

Nelivee continues, "My issue is with the operator of this vehicle."

Winston then responds, "Yes, sir. How can I assist you, sir?"

Nelivee chuckles and says, "Now that's more like it. License and registration."

Winston casts a cautious glance at Lori, signaling with a subtle nod toward the glove compartment. Lori promptly opens it, and a small light shines, revealing the registration document resting on the surface. She leans across Winston and extends it to the waiting officer.

Winston stutters, saying, "My license is in the armrest."

Nelivee dons a devious grin and says, "I like this part."

Winston hesitates and asks, "May I?"

Nelivee, slightly rocking from side to side, replies, "Go right ahead."

Winston lifts the armrest and begins searching. After a moment, he retrieves his wallet and from it, he removes his I.D., and hands it over to the officer, who takes it and shines his flashlight on it.

"You were driving pretty fast on my highway. Where are you and, uh... Miss Lee going in such a hurry?" Nelivee accuses.

Hesitantly, Winston replies, "We were looking for a hotel for the night. We'll be back on the road in the morning."

Nelivee inquires, "Where are you headed?"

Winston quickly answered, "North, to Chicago… Sir."

He guesses, "So, I assume that you are going to stay at Vernon's for the night?" Winston slowly nodded his head up and down.

Nelivee continues, "I tell you what. Since you're a guest in these parts, I'll call Vernon and get y'all a room ready."

The officer stands up, walks away from the car, and pulls out his cell phone. He makes a call. Winston didn't move an inch; the window was still open with rain pouring in all over him.

Lori leans over to Winston, "This guy is mega-weird. Why would he call and book a room for us?"

Nelivee returns with news, "You're good to go! Here is your license and reg." He taps the top of the car, "Go on now. Vernon's waiting. By the way, y'all are in room 301. I'll follow you over."

Winston takes his credentials, exchanging a worrisome glance with Lori. He quickly rolls up the window as the Officer leaves and returns to his cruiser. In the back seat, Winston digs into his bag, pulling out a T-shirt to wipe down the interior door and himself.

Next, he reaches for his black hoodie, removing his wet shirt before donning the hoodie.

With alarm in her voice, she says, “We cannot go there!”

He shrugs, “Apparently, We don’t have a choice.”

Winston pulls off with the police cruiser following closely behind him. Winston keeps a close watch on the speedometer, making certain that he drives below the speed limit to the hotel. Finally, the rain stops, and the Vernon County Suites marquee sign can be seen lit up down the road.

Winston and Lori pull into the desolate parking lot. They look around with the same uneasy feeling settling in their guts.

Winston can feel the heat from Lori’s eyes on the side of his head. Shaking his head, he comments, “Yeah... I know. Another empty parking lot.”

The cruiser pulls in and parks right next to them. Officer Nelivee cockily exits and marches toward the building.

Vernon Gilbert, the hotel proprietor, awaits the group at the entrance. He’s a tall, lanky White man with a burn scar on his right cheek, dressed in what appears to be vintage nineteen-seventies clothing. He stands in the doorway, casually spitting chewing tobacco on the ground.

Winston and Lori step out of the car, standing beside it with a bag in hand.

Watching the officer walk towards him, Vernon says, “They keep you on the night shift, don’t they?” He spits the brown, slimy snuff onto the asphalt near Nelivee’s shoe.

Nelivee looks down at the spit and slightly steps back.

He giggles, "Well, Vernon... if they didn't, I wouldn't have the pleasure of seeing your ugly face." He then turns and stretches his hand out in the couple's direction.

He says cordially, "Don't be shy... ole Vernon here don't bite. He's got the perfect room ready for you."

Winston and Lori stand still, and yell, "Actually, the rain has let up. I think we're good to get back on the road."

Nelivee quickly responds, "Nonsense. We're here, the room is ready, and besides, I don't think you're fit for the road tonight. That's an order!"

Winston looks at Lori and sighs, and they go in. Vernon and Nelivee trail behind them.

CHAPTER ELEVEN

Moments later, they all stand awkwardly in the lobby, its decor a blend of old Americana and hunting lodge chic. Paintings of dogs and elderly White men occupy chairs, while scenes of plantations adorn the walls.

The largest painting on the wall depicts a group of White men bursting out of a log cabin nestled in the woods. They are in hot pursuit of a tall black greyhound, astonishingly running on two legs, clutching a sheet of music in its mouth. The White men brandish ropes, some fashioned into nooses, and long guns equipped with knives on the ends. Meanwhile, other White men toil in the earth, laying down railroad tracks.

Winston and Lori oddly stare at the painting with a sense of unease. As they can clearly see several black figures trapped beneath the railroad tracks, struggling to free themselves.

On the front porch of the log cabin, an elderly White woman sits in a rocking chair, her hands inexplicably black, meticulously painting a picture. The painting's eerie resemblance to the murals they've been encountering sends shivers down the couple's spines.

They exchange apprehensive glances and instinctively draw closer to each other, their unease mounting.

With his hands in his pockets, Vernon says, “Don’t mind that old ugly stuff. Hundreds of years ago, it used to be the Gilbert family homestead. As the story goes...my great-greats loved helping travelers, so they made it into a hotel. It’s in the Will that I can’t change a God-damn thing.”

Officer Nelivee inches his way closer to Winston and Lori.

He belts out, “Can’t say I blame them. Tradition is a big thing with our people.” Standing next to him now, he reaches out and nudges Winston with his elbow. He continues, “You get it... don’t you, Winston?”

Nelivee gives Lori a sarcastic look and comments, “I know that you understand, Miss…”

Lori quickly replies, “Yang... Doctor Lori Yang.”

Nelivee purposely ignores her title, saying, “Ms. Yang. Your people, they preserve tradition at all costs, and you stick together no matter what… I like that!”

Lori looks at Winston.

Winston interjects, “Thank you for the history lesson, but we really should get to our room.”

Vernon perks up, saying, “Oh yeah... yeah. It’s on the house.”

He walks behind the counter and retrieves a room key that reads “301.” Winston and Lori approach the counter and take the key.

Nelivee informs the group, “Hell... it’s so late, I decided to stay over myself. Rest assured, this will be the safest place in town tonight.”

As Winston and Lori walk away, Lori looks back at him with a scowl on her face. Nelivee waves at her, and she turns away.

He shouts, "Have a good night!" which prompts Winston to turn and look at the two.

Vernon locks eyes with Winston for a moment, his expression filled with pity.

Winston then shifts his attention back to Lori, and the couple continues on to the stairwell.

The climb up to their room feels more like a descent. The nagging feeling in their bellies rears its ugly head once again. When they arrive at the door, it reads "301," but the number three is hanging off, dangling from an old nail near the bottom of the digit.

Under where the three was formerly placed is a faint imprint of the number eight. Winston feels queasy, his nemesis showing its face again only backward.

Lori takes her finger and traces the imprint, saying, "801." "There aren't even eight floors here. I wonder where this door came from."

He puts the key in the door and turns the knob. The hotel room is painted a muted gray. It has a king-sized bed with the typical fare, including a wooden desk and chair. Lori walks in and flops on the corner of the bed. Winston follows and hurries to lock the door and slide a nightstand in front of it.

Then, he goes over to the window and peers out at the parking lot, channeling Malcolm X. He can see his car and the police cruiser. There are no other cars in the lot.

Lori inquires, "How do we get out of here? ...We're on the third floor."

Winston rushes around the room. He checks the bathroom and darts back into the room, saying, "We'll wait until that nut goes to sleep."

Lori asks another question, "And if he doesn't?"

Frazzled, he says, "We'll do what we gotta do! Right now, we're safe. Try and relax."

Lori gets up and clicks the button to turn on the TV. It doesn't come on. She clicks the button again. Once again, nothing.

Excited, Winston says, "Wait...check this out!" He rifles through his bag and pulls out a remote control.

Lori asks with disapproval, "Did you steal that?"

Winston shrugs his shoulders.

He clicks the remote, and the TV comes on. Shc looks amazed. He clicks through several channels, but it's just snow and static, saying, "Aw man…now it doesn't work!"

He hands the remote to Lori, and she keeps clicking.

Winston lays on the bed and closes his eyes.

Suddenly, Winston hears clapping and applause coming from the television.

Opening his eyes, he sits straight up and motions for Lori to stop.

Excited, Winston jumps up and points to the TV, saying, "That's the guy!"

Confused, Lori asks, "What guy?"

Winston shushes her and replies, "Dell Ferrell."

They both sit on the bed and start to watch.

On the TV, the show plays. In this episode of Dell Ferrell, he is interviewing a man who looks eerily like Malcolm X. However, he is introduced as Minister Walid Abdullah.

Dell asks him, "I know you can't speak for all Black people, but what do you think is their greatest fear?" The Minister crosses his legs and sits up straighter. Saying, "Dell, we have an extraordinary relationship with panic. I think, in general, what scares Black people the most are the horrors that really do happen to us and the heightened paranoia that we are powerless to do anything about it."

He clasps his hands together and goes on, "So, psychologically it's normal to be afraid of, say, going to jail, but Black people have an exaggerated fear of it because for us it's not just going to jail - it's going to jail even though you haven't done anything."

The audience clamors and speaks indistinctly. Dell raises his hand to them to settle them down, saying to his guest, "Go on." The Minister replies, "Thank you. So all of the normal reactive defenses don't work for us. It doesn't matter that you didn't do it - it doesn't matter that you weren't there - you're guilty because you're Black and because they say so."

Dell lights a cigarette and shakes his head in disagreement, commenting, "In a sense...do you all feel that everybody is out to get you?"

The Minister grins and gives a sarcastic chuckle, replying, "Black people have a uniform anxiety brought on by externally manufactured terror. Given the perpetual state of panic we live in, the horror isn't so much what happens to us, it's anticipating the horrors of what we think could happen to us. Because it often does!"

Dell's eyes beam with delight as he smokes his cigarette, saying, "That's a heavy weight to carry around moment after moment, day after day. It's a wonder that you all have not gone mad!"

The audience claps.

He continues, "Let me ask this, When...or maybe how do you live life between all of those landmines? These things that you've mentioned here tonight, is it possible that just a few of you feel this way?"

The Minister looks at Dell with deadpanned eyes declaring, "More broadly, I think Black people have a deep fear of being exactly what the word Nigger portrays. However, this mentality is not of our own doing.

"We are not the innately savage and depraved monsters you claim us to be." He takes a breath, "As far as America goes, the African-American is a fabricated idea that deserves less than nothing. Your concern is that we have consistently refused your painstaking efforts of converting us into Niggas!"

Winston gets riled up while watching the interview, but Lori's expression and body language show that she's flustered and panicky. She clicks the remote and turns off the TV. Jumping up, he screams, "Why did you do that? Didn't you hear what he was saying? Doesn't that mean anything to you?"

Lori exclaims, "We live in America, somebody has to run it. Just like the Chinese, we run China and...and the Africans, they run Africa."

Winston shouts, "What…The...FUCK! You have a Psychology Degree. You can't be serious right now?"

Lori musters up some courage and stands up defiantly. She defends her position saying, "Yeah, I am! You have to recognize that White American culture is a real thing. America's default is White because they run it. They got here first, they earned that right to make it their own. People do it all the time."

He sharply says, "Earned the right? You have lost your God-damn mind! I never thought you were this damn blind. Lemme give you a for-real-for-real history lesson." Lori crosses her arms in anger. Winston dives in, "Fuckin' Pilgrims i.e. "White People" are Economic Migrants. That's it...that's all! They migrate for consumption like famished cows. Devouring anything and everything to get the bag. Don't get it twisted."

Lori nods her head. Holds her hands over her face in disbelief. She challenges back, "White people control what's going on in the

United States, and so their culture gets to set the norms. That's the real history! Their culture defines what "American" is and what it means."

Winston angrily slaps the back of his hand in his palm hard over and over in emphasis. "White people have not lived here for thousands of years developing a culture and becoming one with the land. They don't have an indigenous presence. They're newcomers whose fabricated fuckin' culture is a new creation. Just because you strong-arm a land and its people into compliance doesn't make you worthy of cementing a culture."

He paces the floor and continues, "Native Americans, Latinos, and only God knows who else have been here all along. So their central White culture is not a natural, organic development, it's one that's shaped by historical and political events. I'll sum it up in two words... "Conquest and Control."

Emotional, Lori asks, "If you feel so strongly about this, then what the hell are we even doing together? I may not be White but I'm surely not Black. Why aren't you with a Black woman?"

Shocked by her question, he sits down and mumbles asking, "The truth?"

Sobbing, Lori says, "Yes."

Winston admits, "I see death for us...Black people I mean. As you so eloquently put it, White people run this shit. Honestly, I'm in the machine. Even though I have a Black mother and sister, in my mind, their beauty and worth are shrouded with inferior thoughts. Dark skin, big noses, nappy hair, all that shit."

He tears up and goes on, "It's one negative thing after another. Everything about us is an obstacle. From combing our hair to getting a job. Hell, I don't even want to be Black. Not because I hate my people. Not really. It's because life doesn't even consider us in the equation."

He balls up his fists and screams, “Dammit! I’m tired of being scared all the time.”

Lori goes to him and puts her arms around him asking, “So, you’re using me to exit the Black experience? Yeah, I’m not your way out.”

He goes on, “No, not as a way out. I’m with you because I love you.”

Lori chuckles and says, “I hope so because I can’t solve any of those problems. And just so you know, our kids are not going to look White. They’d look more Hawaiian at best!”

Winston grins and replies, “Yeah, I realized that a while ago.”

Lori’s tone becomes serious. “I’m glad we’re managing expectations here. Not to mention, every race has its flaws and issues. You can’t accept my challenges without accepting theirs. I don’t know why I never asked this, but have you ever dated a Black woman before?”

Winston nods yes, saying, “It’s challenging because, in my mind, I felt like I was dealing with my struggle times two. It’s tough. I don’t want to have ‘The Talk’ with my kids. When you’re Black, there isn’t just one talk; it’s like chapter one in an ongoing book.”

All of a sudden, there is a knock on the door. Winston and Lori fall silent. The knocks ring out again, but this time louder. Winston leans in and whispers to Lori.

Then, Lori shouts, “Hello?”

A voice replies, “It’s Officer Nelivee. I need to speak with your guy.”

Winston quietly walks to the door, gently pushes the nightstand aside, and positions himself defensively against the door. Lori watches as Winston points to himself and then gestures towards the bathroom. He motions for Lori to respond.

She yells out, "Sorry, I'm in bed, and Winston's in the bathroom. Can he talk to you in the morning?"

Nelivee responds, "No, I need to speak to him right now. Please, just open the door."

Lori looks at Winston with fear in her eyes and shrugs her shoulders. Winston steps away from the door, and they both begin to search for makeshift weapons. They unscrew two chair legs, each with long, gnarly screws at the joints, and stand ready, slightly rocking in a defensive stance.

Nelivee knocks hard again. The knocks turn into a whacking sound as if he's using something sharp to bludgeon the door. Suddenly, the tip of a red axe breaks through. Winston and Lori scream.

Nelivee continues whacking until a hole is big enough for Nelivee to put his arm through. He tries to unlock the door. Winston and Lori charge and attack his arm with their makeshift bats. Nelivee screams. They hit and stab him with the screws. Blood goes everywhere.

In an instant, the attack stops. Winston and Nelivee now face each other through a hole created on either side of the hacked door. With his heart beating out of his chest, Winston felt as if he were experiencing the same fear as Shelly Duvall in "The Shining." They both stand there, bloody and breathing heavily.

Then Nelivee speaks, "I know who you are Mr. Winston Gale...Atlanta Journalist! You damn right MAGA means exactly what you think it means. We gon' get you and all your little friends, too!"

Lori screams, "Stop it…Just stop it!"

He continued, "You can stay South or go North, it don't matter. There ain't no safe place for you people. Y'all tried this a hundred years ago and we almost got you all. Now I'm gonna finish the job!"

Nelivee steps back a few feet and charges at the door, breaking through. Winston and Lori scramble to separate locations in the room. Nelivee chases Winston with the axe, swinging repeatedly but missing. He hacks at the desk and walls. Nelivee swings again and, unfortunately, makes contact with Winston. Winston lets out a long and agonizing scream.

He cuts Winston on the side of his upper right arm. He's bleeding and covers the wound with his hand. Nelivee continues to give chase. They move about the room like predator and prey. Lori hides behind furniture to avoid Nelivee. The dance isn't over, Nelivee swings the axe and Winston swings his stick.

Winston yells, "Why the fuck are you all like this? I bet you don't even know. It's just who the fuck you are!"

Lori makes her way to Winston as the men remain squared off.

Nelivee laughs maniacally saying, "You don't get it, do you? It's simple. We do what we do cause we can! 'Can' turns into will, 'Will" turns into tradition, and 'Tradition' turns into 'Laws.'"

He lets out an exhausted breath, "Why do you think you Niggers take all them pills?"

Surprise Winston asked, "Pills…What?"

Nelivee pokes himself on the temple with his index finger repeatedly, saying, "You sick in the head. You got Drapetomania! Ya'll keep trying to get off the plantation. I'm here to tell you, it ain't never gonna happen!"

Winston shouts, "Drapetomania…What the hell?"

Lori screams, "This is a nightmare…Please…just let us leave!"

As they square off, Winston focuses on Nelivee's badge. The number on the badge reads "433". Shouting at Nelivee, "You're fucking insane!"

Nelivee responds, "As far as I'm concerned, Niggers ain't born with birth certificates, y'all are born with rap sheets!"

Full of rage, Winston demanded to know, "Since you're being so open and honest right now. Where did hundreds of thousands of Black people go? You can't hide that many people."

Nelivee jabbed, "OK…all right. Well, here you go. They DEAD...DEAD...DEAD! We buried all them spooks under the railroad tracks. Did you know that the Tracks are privately held properties? Not even the government can touch 'em. Yo' PEOPLE is buried under the tracks all over the U.S." He belts out into sinister laughter.

Winston angry and wincing from pain replied, "You know what Muthafucka...Fuck you and your traditions. Your years of terrorism end tonight!"

Winston raises his stick, Nelivee raises his axe and they both swing. They make contact. Nelivee hits Winston in the leg. Winston hits Nelivee in the side. Then the lights suddenly go out. Lori hears a jumble of fighting, screaming, and multiple footsteps, and then the devastating sound of a gunshot goes off.

Lori screams.

Someone runs across the room and the lights come on. Winston is sitting on the floor leaning up against the bed covered with blood. Officer Nelivee is face-down on the floor with the back of his head blown out. Bright red blood is splattered all over his white hoodie and Vernon Gilbert is standing over Nelivee's body holding a gun.

Lori is frightened and is standing near the door by the light switch.

Vernon Gilbert calmly says, "I'm tired of this shit! And fuck this motherfucker!"

Vernon spits the brown snuff directly on Nelivee.

Winston looks up and at Vernon, realizing that he's wearing glasses and they are clean and clear.

Winston muttered, "Sir, he was trying to—"

Vernon cut him off saying, "I know what he was trying to do. They been coming over here and doing it for years. My family, too. He adjusted his glasses and continued, "Black people ain't never done nothing to me. Shit, y'all ain't never done nothing to nobody, not really. Hate ain't no way to live but it's a helluva way to die."

Vernon looks down at Nelivee as Lori runs over to help Winston up.

He motions to them, "Go on...get out of here. I'll clean this up." Then he asked, "By the way. You say your last name is Gale?"

Winston nods, "Yes."

Vernon continues, "I've heard that name before from my grandparents. They used to talk about the people who made it out. If your grandma's name was Nora Gale from Georgia, then she made it out. Sorry to say…your grandpa didn't."

Winston lowers his head.

Lori says, "Babe, let's get out of here while we can."

They grab their bags and the remote. Lori helps Winston hobble out of the hotel room.

They both get into the car and drive away.

While they are on the road, Lori provides some welcomed information, "By the way, I think I figured out the music notes on the murals. The notes make words, not music. They spell out safe-haven locations for Black travelers."

During the drive, she explains all the details. After some time on the road, they pass a sign on the highway that reads, "Welcome to Indiana."

CHAPTER TWELVE

After entering Indiana, Winston and Lori pull into a bustling burger joint. They eat burgers as Lori breaks down in detail how the musical codex works, explaining, "Depending on where you are," she points to a fugue symbol, "this corresponds with an alphabet or a number. If a number symbol is next to an alphabet symbol that represents N, S, E, or W - it's telling you what direction to go and how many miles.

Lastly, it spells out names of people or businesses. It really is ingenious. There's a lot more to it. I'm putting it all together in my notes."

Winston grins and replies, "Like a puzzle, huh? Guess we didn't need to make that stop for a puzzle book."

Lori giggles and takes a bite of her burger.

Winston flips through the music book and says, "Isn't it amazing that Black people have to do all of this to navigate through America?"

With a full mouth, Lori looks up at him, wanting to reply but thinking better of it.

She thought to herself, "Is it always going to be like this? There doesn't seem to be any room for me."

Winston lays down the book and continues to enjoy his meal. Lori just couldn't get past the aching feeling that her life would now be filled with an imaginary pursuit of the "White Monster." To her, White people were just as much of a monster as anyone else desperately trying to hold on to power.

She took a big gulp of water and said, "No one is immune to bigotry. I—"

Winston cut her off mid-sentence. "I'm not saying that. I'm just making a factual point. We are sitting here deciphering a 400-year-old code so Black folks can move about the cabin. We have a particularly septic situation that requires an amputation of some sort."

Winston's rant was beginning to fall on deaf ears.

Lori mindlessly gnaws on a French fry while he sinks deeper and deeper into his mania. Lori loves Winston despite her family being staunchly against their union. She often thinks that she stays with Winston out of spite for her parents' traditional ways.

Recalling the last time she visited her parents, Lori's father was sitting in his favorite chair watching the news while Lori was in the kitchen, drinking tea with her mother. A pot of traditional Chinese soup was on the stove, cooking.

Lori sips and says, "I'm sorry I haven't been by as much lately."

Her mother responds sharply, "You're too busy with Winston to remember your real family."

Lori sets her cup down, defying her mother's words. "Mamma? That's not true," she says.

Her mother glances at her husband, frowning, and shouts, "Jun Bao... Your daughter is here."

Her father sighs without taking his attention from his program on television. He says in broken English, “Is she alone?”

Lori’s mom stands up from the table and stirs the soup. She nods her head, saying, “He’s still not over it.”

Just then, her father stands and toddles off to the bedroom. He never once looks back to acknowledge Lori.

A door slams shut with a loud thud.

Lori looks on, shocked, and lowers her head.

Shaken, Lori asks, “Why does he do this?”

Her mother coldly replies, “Lori… this is not new. He’s been like this ever since you started dating Winston. Three years and counting.”

Lori tears up, saying, “And you wonder why... Whatever.”

She pauses and goes on, “I really wish you guys would take the time to get to know him.”

Her mother continues to nonchalantly stir her soup. “Your father feels like you don’t respect our traditions. We didn’t come all the way to America for our only daughter to spit on our customs. We want better for you.”

Her mother reaches into the cabinet and pulls a container of seasoning out, sprinkling it in the soup and taking a taste.

Lori stands and walks over to the stove, asking, “Why don’t you and Poppa like Black people?” Ignoring Lori’s question, she sighs and asks, “Why did you come here, Lori?”

Lori asks, “Can’t I come and see my family?”

Her mother sarcastically replies, “It’s good to know that we’re still your family.”

Lori implores her, “Mamma, give it a chance. Give him a chance.”

Her mother looks at Lori strangely, commenting, “You know, there’s an old Chinese proverb that I love: A hundred no’s are less agonizing than one insincere yes. Soon, you will understand that it is better to be with what you know, than who you know.”

Lori throws her hands in the air, grabs her jacket and her purse, and storms out without saying a word.

On her way out of the house, she decides to exit through the garage. She presses the button to lift the garage door, and light floods in, revealing boxes stacked against the walls. Curious, she goes over to inspect them.

The boxes have handwritten names on them in black marker. Some read “La Ling,” her mother, and some read “Jun Bao,” her father. They are neatly grouped together.

Then Lori notices several boxes off by themselves next to the garbage can. She walks closer to them and reads the solitary name written on them, “Lori.”

She leans against the wall and tears up, then slides down and sits on the floor, sobbing.

Lori is snapped back to reality by Winston’s voice, calling out her name. He asks, “Are you okay?”

She replies, “Yeah… just thinking.”

Winston suggests, “How about we get out of here and test out your code-breaking skills? Let’s try a safe haven hotel.”

Lori forces a smile and agrees.

The couple hits the road for a “Tour De Fugue”. They make their rounds as they work their way through Indiana. On their first stop, they arrive in front of a whimsical yard filled with colorful flowers. A Black woman steps out and waves them into an elegant Victorian home.

They stayed a night and then went on to the next. A small storefront building with a diner on the main level was filled with the smiling faces of Black people having a good time. Everything glittered in the sunlight and felt warm to Winston's heart. Lori steps out at the welcoming sight, filled with oohs and ahhs. Winston smiles as he joins her.

In one of the marked safe-haven locations, Winston and Lori found themselves sharing a meal with an elderly Black man. Plates of food rest on tray tables, and they eat and engage in conversation, exchanging stories over dinner.

As the evening progresses, their host leans slightly toward Winston and slides a folded note across the table. Lori can't help but watch their open secret with a mixture of curiosity and concern.

Thinking to herself, "Here it is, once again, he's making me feel irrelevant. I feel like an 'other'." The stress is taking its toll on her.

Across from her, the man motions to Winston not to open it at that moment. With a nod of understanding, Winston carefully accepts the note and folds it, tucking it into his wallet.

Back on the road somewhere in Indiana. A chime rings out on the dash of Winston's car.

He whines, "Geez… It's time to fill up again." Lori sulks and dismisses his concerns. The lights of a gas station can be seen from the highway; Winston changes lanes and veers onto the off-ramp.

He pulls into the 'Go-Low Gas Station,' and as he does, a White family pulls out at the same time. Winston peers into the car to see a two-year-old little girl in the back seat who stares at him. She's wearing a tiny white hoodie. Her eyes follow Winston intensely as they pull away.

Shaking his head, he mumbles, “She’s dangerous and doesn’t even know it. A fuckin’ atomic bomb in a diaper.”

Winston brings his attention to Lori, who is staring out of her window. Winston snaps his fingers, singing, “Earth to Lori... Earth to Lori.”

She looks over at him.

He continues, “You’ve been awfully quiet the last few miles. What are you thinking about?”

Lori mildly shakes her head as if to indicate “Nothing.”

Winston snaps, “Well! I don’t need a psychology degree to know that’s a lie.”

She replies, “I was thinking about how you risked both of our lives just to ‘maybe’ find out what happened to some people that you don’t even know.”

He shouts, “Don’t know them? They’re my people!”

Appalled, Lori charged back, “Winston…you don’t care about yourself, and you definitely don’t care about me!”

Winston’s eyes widen and he replies, “Here we go again. We been through this already!”

Lori sighs and asks, “Did you know that in October of 1871, in Los Angeles, Chinese people were the victims of one of the largest mass lynchings in the history of the United States? The largest to this day! We represented roughly 10% of the population in California and a full quarter of the State’s workforce.” Winston sits quietly.

She goes on, “I would never... ever, take you on a quest to revisit those horrors for verification’s sake.”

Winston slowly nods in agreement and comments, “I hear you. The problem is, the Chinese are not still hanging from trees. Whenever I see a strange fruit... it’s Black.”

He rolls his eyes and looks out the driver's side window. Frustrated, Lori frowns, gets out of the car, and slams the door. She walks toward the gas station's mini-market.

Before she enters the store, a silver minivan pulls up to a pump next to them. It's filled with a family of Chinese people. Four of them get out and head towards the mini-mart. They approach Lori and have a conversation with her. The expressions on their faces are blank, including Lori's.

Winston's stomach churns as he watches the exchange from across the parking lot. They all look back at Winston and walk together into the store. Two young children and an elderly woman stay in the minivan. They look at Winston with irrelevance. He looks back at them. Uncomfortable, Winston gets out and begins to pump gas.

As he pumps, Lori and the group of Chinese strangers stand together talking at the checkout line. He cocks his head and continues to look on. Lori pays for her items. She walks out of the gas station with the strangers quietly in tow. Winston finishes pumping gas and leans on the car watching Lori walk toward him.

To his shock, Lori walks to the passenger side back door and gets her bag and closes the door. She stands for a moment and looks at Winston, resolutely, saying "I'm leaving with them. I'll leave you my book. Just pay attention to the music notes. The safe places are marked."

Winston moves toward her, attempting to block her path. Lori pauses, meets his gaze briefly, and then, without saying a word, sidesteps him and continues toward the minivan.

Winston stands there with hunched shoulders and outstretched hands as Lori takes her place in the front passenger seat of the Chinese family's minivan.

Winston hurries over to their vehicle, bending slightly to reach the open window where Lori is seated. However, Lori remains resolute, staring straight ahead through the windshield, deliberately ignoring Winston.

Winston shouts, “Where are you going? You don’t even know these people.”

Surly, she responds, “That’s rich!”

Winston asked, “So, you’re just going to leave me on the road like this?”

Lori turns and looks at Winston and says, “Did you know that the entire discipline of Psychology can be summed up in one quote?”

Confused, Winston asks, “Quote...what are you talking about?”

She continues, “When you understand the nature of a thing, you know what it’s capable of. I understand you now.”

Everyone in the car simultaneously turns their gaze toward Winston. Then, in perfect unison, they redirect their attention forward. The minivan pulls away, with all occupants looking straight ahead.

Winston’s anxiety takes over his entire body because he swears that he can hear the audio of Bruce Lee fighting the entire Dojo in “Fist Of Fury” as the vehicle disappears down the road.

Not a word is uttered by Lori’s new companions as they roll down the highway.

Internally, she wrestles with the complex feelings of losing Winston and the glory of winning her fight.

Winston stands in the spot where Lori had pulled off, dumbfounded.

That’s when a 2011 silver Hyundai Azera pulls in. It drives up to a pump across from him, and a woman gets out, looking his way. She exits the car and smiles, saying, “Cheer up!”

Winston looks up, points to himself, and offers a weak grin.

She continues, "Yeah, you! It's not the end of the world. I had that same look a few weeks ago but look at me now. I'm going to Texas to start a new job."

Winston smiles and agrees, "I suppose you're right. I'm starting a new job as well in Chicago."

The woman exclaims, "Wow! That's where I'm from. If you can make it there, you can make it anywhere. Have a safe trip!"

He replies, "Yeah... you too! I'm Winston Gale, by the way. Have a safe trip as well."

The woman smiles and introduces herself, "Nice to meet you, Winston. My name is 'Sandra Bland.'"

She smiles again and strolls into the gas station.

Winston gets into his car and pulls away, disappearing into the darkness as he continues his journey to Chicago.

The Black Toyota cruises down the highway, traveling from one Indiana town to the next. Winston uses Lori's notes in her music book to decipher a few more safe places to eat and rest.

As he makes the stops, he shares the pages from the book with various Black people on the way. Many do not know that they are part of this historic mythology, and they are glad to officially mark the outside of their homes and businesses with the fugue notes from Lori's book.

Winston is on the last leg of his journey, stopping at a safe-haven hotel in Gary, Indiana. He mills around the room, still reeling from Lori's unexpected departure. His anxiety causes him to pace the floor for hours. At some point, it subsides, and he's able to eat and get some rest.

During the night, he turns on the TV and is once again visited by the Dell Ferrell show. This time, he's interviewing a Black woman by the name of "Olivia Angelo." She appears to be in her mid-thirties and is dressed in '70s-style attire.

She exudes the energy of Afeni Shakur or maybe even a young Shirley Chisholm. The camera moves in close to Dell and his guest.

Dell asks smugly, “Wouldn’t it be easier if Black people would just blend in and go along with the systems of America?”

Olivia sternly questions, “You mean ‘Assimilate’. You, Whites, don’t want ‘Assimilation’, not really. What you want is forced compliance. But, for the sake of this conversation, I’ll stay focused on the issue at hand. Nature gives every living organism the ability to adapt and blend in with its environment. Our skin is no exception, given enough time and pressure.”

The audience grumbles.

She went on, “So if Black people agreed to this... travesty, how would you tell us apart from yourselves? Your people would fall in love and mate with the “Faux Snows”. You would mate until eventually, everyone would look really, really White. But, herein lies the problem. You people hate everybody and everything. You’d find something to discriminate against even when everything looks like you. War is what you choose to make when you feel restless, and you are infinitely restless.”

For the first time, Winston voluntarily turns the television off. Once again, his anxiety wells up in his chest and head, causing various flashbacks of Harlow saying “No MOOR Rooms.” He reflects on Denise, trapped in the basement, being tortured out of her Blackness, and the barbecue cannibals with a penchant for “Dark Meat”.

He stands in front of the mirror with the pill bottle in his hand, staring at it. He opens the bottle and closes it without taking a pill. His urges and fears bring him back to the bottle until he takes another good look at himself in the mirror. Finally, he screams, “NO MORE!” and he flushes the pills down the toilet.

CHAPTER THIRTEEN

The melody of Don Shirley's "The Lonesome Road" flows from Winston's open window as he drives, focused on the road ahead. Suddenly, the words that he's been longing to see appear into view. A green road sign advertises, "Welcome to Illinois, Land of Lincoln." Shortly after that, another sign reads, "Interstate 55, Stevenson Expressway." Winston is giddy with delight, thinking, "I made it!"

As he drives, he stares at all the tall buildings and iconic landmarks along Lakeshore Dr. at 22nd St. He passes under it. Winston remembers that he made a list of his own, of ten places he wants to see or eat at once he makes it to the Windy City. So, he decides to take a detour before going to his new apartment. This list reads:

1. Mosque Maryam
2. The Obamas' House
3. Muhammad Ali's House
4. Farrakhan's House
5. Promontory Point

6. The Museum of Science and Industry
7. The Bean
8. Harold's Chicken
9. Beggar's Pizza
10. Home of the Hoagy

Winston stops at as many places as he can, gorging on one delicacy or another while he parks in front of his chosen landmarks. Once he has his fill, it's back on the road to see his new apartment. Another Bee-Bee's Honey delivery truck passes Winston on the highway.

Again, he does not notice it. He is busy tuning his radio to the local stations. Settling on one, he enjoys the lively atmosphere of the North.

Winston arrives in front of a tall, upscale apartment building situated on Lakeshore Drive, overlooking the lakefront on Chicago's Southside. The building is contemporary and impeccably maintained. He gazes upward and breaks into a smile.

The first thing he does is exit his car and go to the trunk to open it. He stood, staring for a moment, realizing that all he had left from the beginning of the trip was a single duffle bag. And there next to it was another tiny bag that was Lori's. He sighed and picked up both.

He boards the elevator and reaches the ninth floor, carrying his belongings and food haul to the door. His apartment number reads, "9-F." He grins and opens the door. The unit is spacious with clean white walls, hardwood floors, and floor-to-ceiling windows. The living room is filled with boxes and wrapped furniture. Several boxes are marked "Books."

Winston walks over to the boxes and uses his key to cut the tape. Inside, the books are stacked neatly. He sits in the corner of his sofa, holding a book in his hand; the cover reads, "The Negro Safe Traveler's Guide." Winston taps the cover, commenting, "Could've really used you!" He gently places it on top of the box.

Next, he opens his duffle bag and retrieves Lori's music book. He takes a moment to flip through it, a smile lighting up his face. He carefully places the music book inside the box with the rest of his important tomes.

When he's done, he decides to explore his new place further.

He walks into the kitchen and glances at the fridge. A large note is taped to it, reading, "Hey Bro, guess you're having a really good time. I've been calling you for days but no answer. Give me a ring when you get this. P.S. Tell your Super thanks again for leaving this note for me."

Winston tapes the note back to the fridge, mumbling, "Yeah... a really good time."

He walks out of the kitchen and stands in front of the windows in the living room. Being on the ninth floor, he has a clear view of Lake Michigan. He stares at the lake like a burden has been lifted off of his shoulders.

Winston wastes no time in securing a new phone. He stops at the local We-Mobile and picks up a new phone with the same phone number. He hopes to receive a message or two from Lori or Mike. However, once he activates his phone, he is flooded with messages from everyone but them. There are texts and emails from an unknown sender sharing a screenshot of an Atlanta Police interview regarding a missing person, "Lilbert Lewis." Winston gasps, covering his mouth. He has no one to call; he doesn't know any of his friends or family.

The only thing he can think to do is to respond to the text and email addresses, but no one replies. He swears that he will investigate and find out what might have happened to his friend; there has to be a clue somewhere.

That following Monday, it's time for Winston to meet his new boss and see where he will be working. "The Chicago Blaze Publication" is nestled in the middle of a residential area called Hyde Park. It's a stone's throw from the University of Chicago and a grade school named Charles Kozminski.

Winston is intrigued by that name, Kozminski, because during his research on the school and the area, he can find no references to who he was or any ties to the community. It's as if a prestigious-sounding fictitious name was just slapped on the facade of a vast multicultural community learning institution without any regard.

Walking into the Chicago Blaze, the air feels different to Winston. Although the comings and goings are the same, the ambiance feels light, inclusive, and jovial. Winston waits for the elevator, with people from all walks of life greeting each other as they start their day.

When he reaches his floor, he exits the elevator along with several other people who are headed in the same direction. He takes a few more steps and looks at the banner over the door that reads, "Our motto is... Truth, Facts, and Courage." He smiles and walks in.

His first stop is the receptionist's desk, announcing, "Hi, my name is Winston Gale and I'm here to see Marguerite Turner."

The young lady checks her computer and replies, "Yes, Mr. Gale. Have a seat, someone will be out to get you."

The lobby is filled with framed articles with large mounted pictures of famous people or events peppered throughout as well. The decor is vibrant with streaks of red, orange, and yellow; he assumes it references the flames in the name of the company.

As Winston wanders to choose a seat, the clicks of many keyboards can be heard amongst the loud conversations being had in the bullpen.

Before he can plant himself down, he hears the raspy voice of a woman calling his name, "Mr. Gale I presume?" He pops right back up, "Yes, that is correct!"

That's when he sees her, a beautiful silver-haired older woman in a stylish ensemble. She is wearing a chunky tribal necklace around her neck with a set of pearl earrings.

She says, "I'm Marguerite Turner. It's so nice to have you. Follow me to my office so that we can chat." Winston rushes to follow her.

Her office is immaculate and filled with images of relevant historical events that have taken place with people of color in Chicago and around the globe.

After she sits down at her desk, she says to Winston, "I was raised on the low-end of Chicago by my grandmother. I'm sure it will surprise you to know that we lived right across the street from the El Rukn Gang's clubhouse, which, at the time, was on 39th and Cottage Grove.

There was a wide grassy median that separated the north and south traffic lanes, so we were 'technically' a safe distance away from the activities." Laughing out loud, she declares that, "Friday nights were a spectacle to behold."

Winston lowers his bag to the floor and comments, "No... no, I did not know that."

She goes on, "It was so commonplace that my brothers and I had no idea that there was danger afoot. Maybe it was because my grandmother, her name was Alyce, by the way, made an event out of it. Like going to see pugilists fight at Caesar's Palace or something."

Winston listens on in awe.

She asks, "You may be wondering why I'm telling you this.

It's because after being released from the physical grasp of American bondage, so to speak, we instituted a bondage of our own out of necessity, as ignorant as it sounds.

But out of that wayward struggle came people like Huey Newton, Fred Hampton, Stokely Carmichael, and even myself. We all spoke out against the establishment in our own respective ways."

Winston is all smiles with what he is hearing.

She goes on, "Now all of that brings me to you. You have proven to be one of us, which is why you're here. You spoke truth to power, and that put you on my radar!"

Winston steeples his hands in a prayer pose while slightly bowing, "Thank you. I am really honored."

Marguerite stands and walks around her desk and sits on the corner of it near Winston. She looks him eye to eye and declares, "I'm not blowing smoke up your ass either. That article damning MAGA was stellar and precise. It sliced at the jugular of Lady Liberty herself. I promise, if you would've boarded a flight to New York the day the article was published, you would have seen blood flowing from her neck!"

Winston nervously raises his brows saying, "I hope that I can keep that momentum."

In response, she stands up, rests her hand on his shoulder, and replies, "You will, son. I have no doubt."

She then walks to the door and beckons him, "Come... let me show you to your new office."

As they walk, Marguerite gives him the lay of the land, pointing out who is who and what they do.

When they reach the chatty Bullpen, they stop, and she claps her hands loudly in the air to command silence.

She announces, "Ladies and gentlemen, this is Winston Gale, our new investigative journalist. For those who do not know, he was the columnist who wrote "*Make America Great Again...The Battle Cry of Sleeper Racists*."

Suddenly, the entire office stands up, some individually and some in clusters, and begins to clap until the thunderous applause echoes off the ceilings.

While the room roars, she leans over to Winston and whispers in his ear, saying, "I told you, you're in the right place to be great!"

Winston is an instant success for Chicago Blaze. He investigates and writes about the unseen dealings in politics, finance, and the educational system. His stories are hard-hitting, truthful, and call for action.

However, there is one story that he has not written about: The Great Migration, his missing great-grandparents, and his experience traveling North. He doesn't want to lose the credibility and status he's just acquired.

He decides to keep the story under wraps until the time is right. For now, he wants to make the most of this improved situation that he now enjoys.

He often thinks about Lori; sometimes he even dials her number but thinks better of it before clicking to call. He realizes that he might not have been the best person for her, nor she for him. He hopes that she is okay and maybe she has continued on to Chicago, and they will meet in the most random of places. Just maybe.

After Winston is settled in his new office, Marguerite sits at her desk flipping through a photo album that is filled with photos of Black men and women.

Below their images are their names, dates, and other particulars. She grins at one of the photos, which is of a man named “LaBob Harrison,” then she closes the book and leans back in her chair.

Marguerite’s story is more complicated than she lets on. She is married to a renowned geneticist who faded from the public eye forty years ago.

He became reclusive in their sprawling 20,000 square-foot home in Kenwood, which is a genuine urban French Chateau-styled castle located at 49th and Drexel Blvd. Her husband, Dr. Janus Harper-Turner, whom she affectionately refers to as “Harp” continues on with his research, utilizing a portion of their home to work in.

Janus is in his early seventies and is tall and extremely fit for his age. He dons a bald head and a striking silver-white mustache and beard.

It is rare that anyone, including his wife, sees him out of a lab coat and a pair of stylish gabardine pants.

That evening, after introducing Winston to her team, Marguerite comes home excited about the stories that her new investigative journalist wrote. She is so preoccupied in thought that she does not see her husband sitting in a reclining chair in the living room.

Janus clears his throat, and Marguerite stops in mid-step to see him there as if he were waiting for her.

Startled, she asks, “Harp, what are you doing there?” She jokes, “I haven’t seen you above sea level at this time of day in years.”

He frowns at her with a perturbed look on his face and says, “I don’t think that we should continue with this insane effort of yours.

It's been ten years now, and we have most certainly become a cautionary tale."

Marguerite stops in her tracks and spins around towards Janus, saying, "Have you forgotten the mission of this, as you call it, 'insane effort'?" She walks over to him and firmly states, "There is no stopping until we have justified America!"

Janus roars, "What we have done has larger ramifications than just leveling the playing field, ramming square pegs into round holes. It does not work and should not be!"

Marguerite snidely asks, "Doesn't it?"

She takes a seat and informs him, "I had lunch with one of those 'square pegs' just last week. He was a fine specimen and an awesome addition to the team."

Janus scoffs, "I'm almost certain that he doesn't feel that way."

She replies, "I grant you that. Fortunately, like the others, he doesn't remember much from before. It was a conversation that needed to be had after he completed his conversion."

Janus says, "I warned you about reintegrating too soon. I said if you did, their mental limbo will cause undue attention and questions."

She follows that with a giggle.

"What's so funny?" he asks.

She replies, "I told him his name was "LaBob" and he was surprisingly happy to learn that!"

He angrily reprimands her, saying, "Marguerite…this is not a game!"

Still giggling, she replies, "Harp, I got this. We haven't had one go bad yet."

Crossing his arms and then his legs, he asks, "So what did you disclose to him?"

Marguerite smiles and says, “The God’s honest truth. He wanted to know why it is that only Black people can see racism and what exactly do White people want from us, overall. So, the conversation went something like this”:

She says, “Racism is a special kind of horror because it was cultivated for the purpose of annihilating one’s soul, culture, and purpose while maintaining their husk for repetitive use. It’s not just one thing, it is a fluid and morphing entity that can be seen, felt, and touched by anyone who dares to look.

We talk, write, and preach about racism because it never goes away. It just mutates and is allowed to live another day, only to return as something new. Also, America has a fascination with automatons for very concerning reasons and it is two-fold.” Janus motions for her to carry on.

She continued, “I said, first it’s their ongoing obsession for a programmable human presence who is an empty shell. They see this as the future. Secondly, they’re desire to own things that are void of independent thought, emotions, and nerve endings that can realize pain. Something that cannot process being overworked, abused, and uncompensated. Just think about that for a second, that sounds eerily reminiscent of slavery, doesn’t it?”

She pauses for a moment, then says, “And let’s not forget the thousands of micro-aggressions that we have to suffer. We can’t wear our natural hair; our naturally voluminous bosoms and derrières make them uncomfortable, even while hidden under blazers and flowing skirts.

If a Black man crosses his arms, then he is treated like a threat. If a Black woman asserts herself, then she’s seen as angry and dangerous. Hell, our children can’t even play with neon orange water pistols without being shot by the police. Shit… where can we be Black?”

Janus asks, “Are you done?”

“No!” she exclaims, and sighs, “Then he asked about educating others about racism and oppression.”

Janus utters, “Well…”

She goes on, “I told him that our history is being whitewashed to the point of parody and confusion, which, by design, is their plan. Whippings were just love taps to keep us from going off the straight and narrow. The rapings of our women and little girls were a public service to assist the Black with having a family of their own if their Black husbands were sterile. You know how they can water down water into a Fairytale.”

Janus gives her a sarcastic look.

Marguerite acquiesces to his disapproval, saying, “Ok…ok, without the comedy routine, I told him that if they are not going to teach historical facts in schools about racism and slavery, then their books should come with a disclaimer on the cover that says “For Entertainment Purposes Only.”

Shaking his head, he solemnly says, “This is not what the Metraxicide was for.”

Marguerite stands up and walks over to Janus and sits next to him. She says, “Metraxicide can still work the way it was intended; it just needs a little more work. But right now, it works perfectly for melaninizing white people to increase the population of Black people. What you have developed is a game-changer! Are we going to have some failures?… Of course.

Are we going to have some of those failures vote Republican and against their own interest…Yep! But until that happens, let’s focus on the bigger picture, and that’s becoming the real majority in the United States so that we can change all of that. Besides, If everyone is Black then no one is on Zencitravmasi. You know exactly what that does to our people.”

Janus looks at her, “But there’s no way to deliver the mRNA injections to millions of white people twice a year no less without just cause.”

Marguerite smiles and says, “You, sir scientist, have no faith in Mother Nature. She is guaranteed to present a calamity that will need to be dealt with. It may not happen today, but give it some time. I promise you that there will be a time when thousands upon thousands of our target market will be begging for it!”

CHAPTER FOURTEEN

Several weeks have passed after Marguerite started Winston as her new star journalist. With a little more time on her hands, she decides to catch up with the intake on her pet project at her home. Marguerite sits pensively at her desk, typing in her journal. As she writes, she opens some of her past notes from the beginning of their experiments that detailed the process of reverse engineering blackness in Caucasian people. She reads:

"Once it was understood that every living human being on Earth derived from a Black woman, yes, even non-melanated people, attaching to their leftover seedlings was simple. Then all we had to do was enhance it and allow it to bloom.

This effort of converting white people into "Nouveau Ethnic" was an enormous undertaking. Janus first tested the "Metraxicide" on mice; however, the results that he expected were not as fruitful as the unexpected side effects. The white mice eventually turned into Black mice. He was able to duplicate the results repeatedly. He hid this information from me for years.

He knew me all too well because when I learned of it, I coerced him into human testing. I could tell in his eyes that the scientist in him had to know if it would work, and it did! After years of implementation, we had a formula and a system. Once the conversion had begun, the individuals would need to be housed subversively. There were only two injections needed to complete the process.

Janus' original intent for the "Metraxicide" was to erase the embedded deleterious effects made in Black people due to enslavement. The glomming-on of self-hate, colorism, lack of belief in self or trust in anyone who looks like us, and the effects of Jim Crow which still damage us till this day.

Oddly enough, it focuses on the same parts of the brain that Zencitravmasi affects, except instead of numbing those areas and making us docile, the Metraxicide will override its chemical puppeting and maximize our "King-Gene," freeing us from any mental chains.

However, applications of the Metraxicide in some members who are naturally melanated and have been long-treated with Zencitravmasi have not been able to maintain the functionality of the "King-Gene" for longer than a few months because their brains have been drenched into submission by Zencitravmasi.

Marguerite closes the page and sits in silence for a moment.

Suddenly, her cell phone rings and it is her and Janus's personal assistant, Breona, calling.

She answers, "Good day…" Breona replies, "I have a new volunteer. Can you interview her tonight?" Marguerite replies, "Yes, indeed. Bring her to the rear entrance of the lab at 8:00 pm."

She clicks off the phone and picks up her purse to leave.

On the way out, she stops by Winston's office to check on him. As she stands near the entrance of his office, he is hard at work typing up an article.

Marguerite can see the zeal and determination in his eyes dancing on his computer screen. She enters saying, “Winston, you seem to have settled in nicely!”

He quickly stops typing and comes to attention, saying, “Indeed, Ma’am, it’s going well.”

She asks, “May I ask what you are working on?”

He replies, “Oh yes. I’m sorry... I’m not used to developing my own stories and not having to get them approved first.”

She leans over and comments, “I brought you on as an investigative journalist; that’s your job. I’m just being nosy.”

He pushes his laptop closer in her direction.

Marguerite leans over and squints, then she lets out a loud, “Zencitravmasi... Ahhhh!”

Winston replies, “You think it’s a good subject?”

Nodding her head, she replies, “You have no idea how intrigued I am about the subject matter.”

She places her purse on his desk and takes a seat.

Winston comments, “In all honesty, I’m writing this article because of the experiences I had on the road coming here. I kind of did my own “Great Migration” and went down the roads less traveled to learn what my family and other Black people may have experienced when moving North from the southern states.

Let’s just say, I was grossly unprepared for what I discovered about Zencitravimasi and the South.”

Eyes ablaze, Marguerite replies, “Now that’s a story that I would like to read.”

Winston replies, “I’m not ready yet, but soon.”

Marguerite takes a deep breath and says, “I understand. You will soon learn that you have more allies than you know. Just like you, Janus was curious about how it worked and what it really did as well. A lot of us were born with it in our systems, seeing that it was passed to us from our mothers in the womb."

She uses her foot to reach over and closes the door, saying in a hushed voice, "I don't talk about it much, but my husband, Janus, is a retired Geneticist, and he has been looking into Zencitravmasi for years. You know, they started the research for it in the late '20s."

Winston interrupts, saying, "Funny that you should mention it. I've been going through the timeline, and it's murky about when it was developed."

She asks, "If you have a moment, I can give you a huge leg up on your research?"

He replies, "Yes, I'd love that!"

Marguerite goes on, "The drug was initially created as a medication to cure the plague."

Winston is surprised, "I was told that it was made to treat PTSD and other fear-based anxieties?"

She replies, "That's true too, but this is how it all went down. It all started with rats... It's always rats!"

Winston pulls out a pen and pad and writes feverishly as she speaks.

She says, "Some rich white man and his wife went on vacation overseas, and somehow or another, she became ill. After returning home, she got even sicker, and a doctor was called in to examine her. That's when her husband got the news that she was bitten on her toe by a rat that was infected with the plague."

"As the story goes, her rich husband, sick with grief, funded some scientists in Turkey to find a cure. Unfortunately, cures take a lot of time and money to come about, and she passed. For that matter, so did he."

She stops for a second and digs in her bag for an old, weathered bottle of Zencitravimasi. She gently sets it down on the desk.

Winston looks over in awe to see her name affixed to the label.

She continues, "So after the plague dissipated on its own, the Turks slapped the rich guy's name on a wing of a research facility and kept using rats to develop the drug further to see what it could become.

What they learned is that the rats, sick or not, became docile even when mistreated and shunned. These tiny beasts of burden would be abused, starved, and isolated, and they treated their captors with no disregard or malice. So they packaged it and contacted the American government and sold the rights to the medication to our country."

Dumbfounded, Winston states, "You have got to be kidding?"

She whispers, "Nope, but there's more.

The name, "Zencitravmasi," if you separate the 'i' and the 't,' it spells "Zenci Travmasi," which in Turkish means... wait for it, 'Black Trauma.'"

Winston's mouth falls open.

She smiles and says, "Before you finish your story, let's schedule a time for you to come by my place and meet my husband. And when you do, it's best to refer to him as "Dr. Turner."

She stands up and adds with a humorous tone, "Believe me, it's best for everyone."

Then she walks out the door.

Some Weeks Later...

Winston strolls into a cell phone store and walks up to the counter. A sales associate, Jacy, greets Winston from behind the counter, saying, "Welcome to We-Mobile."

Giving Winston a look, he asked, "Hey…weren't you here a couple of months ago?"

Winston, shaking his head, holds up his cell phone revealing a badly cracked screen.

Replying, "Yeah…I'm back for another repair."

Jacy responds, "No problem. Give me about 20 minutes. I'll take care of that for you."

Winston hands Jacy his phone and comments, "I guess I'll take a quick look around."

Winston steps away from the counter and starts to browse the phones on display. A woman passes by him unnoticed during her first lap around the store. However, as she walks by again, their eyes finally meet.

Raveen Tillson is a stunningly gorgeous Black woman, with ebony-colored skin and wearing a bright yellow sundress.

Now that they have seen one another, she pretends to coyly look at cell phones.

Winston slightly raises his voice saying, "Yellow looks good on you."

Blushing, Raveen looks at Winston and back at the phones and says, "Thank you! I like the way it plays with the darkness of my skin. Yellow makes me feel like a Queen Bee."

Winston shoots her a strange look.

Raven comically huffs and continues, "Well… I guess not."

Winston stutters, "No, I'm...I'm sorry. You look great. I recently learned that I'm deathly allergic to Bees. That's all."

She responds, "Is that right?"

He laughs commenting. "Yeah, it's a long story but maybe I can tell it to you over lunch."

They smile at each other and talk further.

That day, they had lunch in a charming restaurant by the lake. The space was filled with people, all engaged in lively conversations and savoring their meals. During lunch, Winston notices small glass jars of honey on a few of the tables. He frowns as other patrons use the honey to sweeten their food and drinks.

Suddenly, their waitress brings over some complimentary items, one of which is honey. Winston somewhat assertively hands it back to her and wipes his hands with a napkin.

Raveen asks, "What's that all about? Is it the bee thing again?"

Winston calms himself and offers a smile. Saying, "Ah…there was a recall a while back with some honey down south. Just didn't want to take any chances."

Winston quickly changes the subject, and they continue with their day.

Raveen has become a staple in Winston's life. She spends a lot of time at his apartment, helping to unpack boxes and situating furniture. On several occasions, she has come to his office and read one or two of his many articles aloud to him in jest while she prances around his desk.

Even though Winston isn't ready to reveal his personal experience, he does write it down. He titles it "The One That Made It - The Journey North." However, he keeps it under lock and key; not even Raveen knows what happened.

Oddly enough, after Winston met Raveen, his need for medicating with Zencitravmasi left him. As he travels around the city, reminders of his addiction are everywhere. He sees on a number of occasions mothers hand-feeding the poison to their children while they wait at bus stops, and even men tossing back a few pills after a basketball game at the park.

Once he came to grips with what the drug ultimately did, he was never visited by the Dell Ferrell show again, and Winston was able to bring down his anxiety to manageable levels with a better environment and a new love. He and Raveen seemed to have a compatibility that gave them a synergy that he never thought could exist.

Ironically, Raveen's chosen profession complements Winston's in a fitting way. She is a Black History Professor at the University of Chicago and the Director of The Mayflower Resolution Association. She speaks often about the plight of Black people.

They spend most of their nights engaging in deep intellectual conversations or debates. When they aren't doing that, they are cuddled together, watching a show, and sharing a good bottle of wine. This night was no different, with the exception of an unexpected call.

Winston looks at his phone, sits up, and answers, saying, "Hey Mike… How are you?"

He responds, "Brother, I'm good! Are you alone?"

Winston glances down at Raveen and replies, "Sure, let me check my folder."

He excuses himself and goes to his office.

He comments, "I am now. What's up?"

Mike responds, "Per our last conversation, you told me to tell you if I heard from or saw Lori. Well, I have, and man... the shit she's saying is crazy!"

Whispering, Winston replies, "Yeah, I'll bet. Look, this is a longer story than I have time for. Just let her know that if she ever wants to clear the air, I'm ready to give it some closure. I owe her that much."

Mike agrees, "Alright man, make it do what it do. Talk soon."

And the line goes silent.

That following week, Raveen wakes up alone. Winston has already left for work but is nice enough to leave her a note on his pillow. It reads, "I can't wait to see you tonight. Have a great day! - Winston." She smiles as she reads the note. She folds it and places it on her nightstand, in doing so, her fingers run across something imprinted on the back. The impression reads, "Lori's appointment."

She tilts her head with concern but decides to let it go. Thinking to herself, "Lori could be anybody. Maybe a colleague or something to do with a story?" She sticks the note in the nightstand drawer. Looking at the clock, she realizes that she is running late, she springs out of bed and rushes to the office.

Raveen was typically a reserved person, especially in a professional setting. However, as of late, she had been very relaxed and jovial, almost to the point of being effusive."

Her demeanor does not go unnoticed. Her co-worker and friend, Alexis, pulls Raveen to the side for a little friendly interrogation. She quips, "Alright, what's his name?"

Raveen chuckles and gushes, "His name is Winston. We've been seeing each other for a little while now. He just moved here from Atlanta."

Alexis raises an eyebrow, wearing a mischievous grin. "Is that right? Tell me more," she insists, leaning in with curiosity.

Alexis asks, "And what does this Winston do?"

Raveen grins and gushes. "Well, he's an investigative journalist. He's brilliant and has a great sense of humor. Plus, he's really into activism for the Black community in ways that I really admire."

Alexis nods, looking genuinely interested. "Sounds like quite the catch," she remarks with a knowing smile. Then she adds, "Now...tell me the bad stuff!"

Raveen hooks Alexis' arm in hers, and they walk shoulder to shoulder to an empty break room. After they sit down, Raveen confides, "It's nothing bad, but I feel that something went down before he got here. Maybe an ex-girlfriend kinda thing."

Alexis inquires, "Did you ask him about it?"

Raveen shrugs her shoulders, saying, "Yes," while shaking her head "No".

"Well, that's not confusing," Alexis replies with a smile.

Raveen continues, "I don't want to be THAT girl. You know…worried about what was and not what will be."

The break room starts to fill with people talking and moving about. Raveen quickly changes the mood, awkwardly saying, "Great talk! Let's do it again real soon. I've got to get back to writing that speech." She pops up from the table and walks out.

That talk with Alexis seems to activate her curiosity. When Raveen arrives back at her office, she closes the door and conducts an internet search for "Winston Gale." The first thing that amuses her is learning that his middle name is "Ross."

The next thing she discovers is that he shares an address with a Lori Su Yang. Her heart begins to pound heavily. Raveen's finger hovers over the search button, torn between her confidence in not needing to know and her insecurity about wanting to know. Unfortunately, her insecurity wins the fight, and lines and lines of data about Lori Yang fill her screen.

She spends the better part of her morning reading whatever she can find about them both. Somehow, she feels closer to Winston and a little ashamed that she has betrayed his trust.

As she sits staring at a listing with Lori's phone number, Raveen's phone suddenly rings—it's Winston. She quickly clicks her computer off and answers the phone.

In a cheery voice, Winston says, "I miss you already…we're gonna have to do something about that."

Raveen's face beams. "Really…Like what?" He replies, "I don't know, but you just let me worry about that."

Raveen chuckles.

Winston goes on, "I'm calling because I'm going to be late tonight. My boss gave me an offer that I can't refuse. I want to take her up on it while my ideas for the story are still fresh in my head."

She replies, "No problem. I'm working a little late tonight myself. I have a speech to prepare for.

Winston comments, "Okay, talk to you later." Then he ends the call.

Raveen sits staring blankly at her computer screen, then turns it back on to begin writing her speech.

Over at the Chicago Blaze Publication, Winston continued his research on Zencitravmasi. However, he could not get the conversation that he had with Marguerite weeks prior out of his head. He dials her on his mobile, asking if he can schedule an interview with Dr. Turner for that evening after work. Marguerite happily agrees and sets up the meeting for 6:00 p.m.

Winston is thrilled that he will have access to unrivaled information for his piece that was months in the making. His day could not be going better when his phone rings again. Not bothering to look at the caller ID because he assumes that it is

Marguerite calling back with more details for the interview, he answers the phone with a ring in his voice reminiscent of J.J. Walker, saying, “Chello!” The voice on the other end is dry and monotone, replying, “Nǐ hǎo.”

Winston turns white and nearly drops the phone. It bounces around in his hand until finally, he holds it firmly. Placing it up to his ear, he asks, “Lori…is that you?”

She replies, “Yes, it’s me. I didn’t think that I would ever make this call. Especially with how we ended things.”

Winston’s heart races a mile a minute, his mouth as dry as cotton as he searches for the words to speak. He replies, “Lori…I’m so sorry. I messed up. Can you forgive me?”

She says, “I do forgive you, and I have to ask you to forgive me as well.”

He asks, “Forgive you for what?”

She goes on, “You were right, I am being prejudiced against you. I didn’t see it at the time, but I didn’t want to deal with your issues—Black issues. I do love you, but only the parts of you that don’t tread on my identity or make me responsible for yours. It was just easier to screw you and take your mind off of it. And I’m truly sorry for that.”

Winston falls back into his chair, saying, “Well, if we’re being honest, I was being selfish and never considered what you and your ancestors had to suffer through too. We all have lost much at the hands of the White man.”

Lori stays quiet on the other end.

Winston continues, “We don’t have to air the whole thing out now, but let’s keep in touch. A lot has changed, and I would like to talk to you about it.”

Lori replies, “I know. Mike told me. I looked her up online, Raveen is beautiful.”

For the second time this week, Winston sits with his mouth open. Before he can say something, there is a click. Then the line goes silent.

He looks at his phone and then lays it on the desk.

Winston finishes the day in the best way he can. Looking up at the clock, he sees that it's just about 5:00 p.m. His interview with Mr. Turner is just about an hour away, so he packs up his things and heads for the door. On the way out, he feels a sense of déjà vu walking past the bullpen and out to the reception area, much like he had at "The Southern Republic."

However, he can sense the living force of integrity and journalism flowing through the air here. He feels that once this new piece is done, he will receive the accolades he deserves, not the scorn.

Before Winston arrives at the Turners', Marguerite, Janus, and her assistant, Breona, ushers one of the converts through the finalization stages of the process. Janus cleans her arm with a medicated cotton ball and injects the woman with a dose of Metraxicide. The woman attempts to speak but cannot. She smacks and licks her lips as if she were thirsty.

Breona goes over and lays the woman down on the gurney. Subtle changes begin to happen to the woman right before their eyes. Her stringy brown hair begins to wave, and her skin turns to a light brownish tint.

Marguerite comments, "Harp, Winston will be here soon. You should change and receive him in the study. Breona and I will get her into the tank."

Janus replies, "Remember, put it on the schedule that after seventy-two hours, we'll lower the oxygen by twenty percent and raise the temperature to ninety-eight degrees for five days. Also, administer three stabilizer tablets every six hours."

Breona shouts, "Yes, Dr. Turner."

Marguerite responds, "Harp, as I mentioned before, this isn't my first rodeo. I love you, Darling. See you soon."

Janus boards an elevator that carries him to the main floor of the home. Marguerite sighs and says, "All he cares about is the science. What he doesn't understand is that this can change the trajectory of the world forever. We must continue this work at all costs!"

Winston pulls up to the Turners' home, having done a quick internet search beforehand. Learning that this gargantuan stretch of property is one of the grandest mansions in the Kenwood community, is the McGill House. The massively-scaled 'picturesque' mansion was constructed in 1891 as the residence of physician and entrepreneur Dr. John A. McGill.

Winston thinks it apropos that the current owner is not only a doctor but also Black. As he exits his vehicle, he snaps a photo with his cell phone and walks to the stairway.

Upstairs, Janus changes out of his laboratory attire and into proper interview clothing, which consists of a white Oxford shirt, khaki slacks, and a tweed jacket. He shuffles to the study and lays out several science periodicals that prominently display his name before taking his seat behind a massive oak desk. Just then, the doorbell rings, and Janus remembers that his wife is in the lab. He realizes he'll have to abandon his plans of being formally introduced to his guest.

Janus quickly makes it to the door, catching his breath before he opens it. He doesn't want to appear too eager to welcome his visitor into his home. Janus opens the door, offers his hand, and says, "Winston Gale, I presume." Winston smiles and shakes it, replying, "Dr. Turner, it's so nice to meet you!"

Winston is in awe of their home. Dr. Turner leads him to the study and offers Winston a seat. Janus is thrilled to have a guest who isn't a patient or even his wife, for that matter. He starts the conversation by boasting about his achievements and grandstanding about his litany of books. His eagerness is not lost on Winston; however, he loves every minute of being in the presence of such an accomplished man.

During the conversation, Winston presents a voice recorder and a pen and pad. Janus is almost taken aback by the formal nature of the gesture. Winston asks, "Can you share with me a little bit about your research on Zencitravmasi?" Janus obliges him.

The two speak for hours about the nature and the ultimate goal of the medication. Janus describes how he has witnessed newborns born without a whimper or a tear due to the sedative-like properties of Zencitravmasi. He asks, "How could you not recoil from being ripped out of the only world of warmth and darkness into bright light and all-consuming noise without screaming in pain and fear? That's when I knew that the malice was deeper than anyone may have understood."

Winston takes notes as he speaks. He asks another question, "Dr. Turner, are you or have you been on Zencitravmasi?" Dr. Turner pauses, then he answers, "I and my wife have been off of it for years. The stain of that poison is one of the reasons that we never had any children. We didn't want to pass it to them."

Winston nods his head as he writes.

Dr. Turner goes on, "The creation of that dreadful medication marked the beginning of my own research."

Winston innocently replies, "May I ask what that research is?" He pushes the recorder closer to Janus.

Janus instantly looks uneasy. In his excitement, he is now aware that he's said too much and quickly changes the subject. "Look at the time; it's after ten o'clock."

Winston looks around, confused, and says, "I'm so sorry. I didn't mean to keep you so long."

Janus stands and walks over to Winston, replying, "I wouldn't dare say this in front of my wife, but I've been feeling my age. Let's pick this up in a couple of weeks." While packing his things, Winston replies, "Yes, sir... Doctor. Yes, Dr. Turner!" He shakes his hand, and Winston leaves.

When Winston reaches his car, he dials Raveen but gets her voicemail. He leaves a message saying, "You won't believe the night that I just had. The article that I'm going to write next will definitely be one for the history books! See you soon."

Back inside, Marguerite creeps from around the corner and steps into the study where her husband is, coyly saying, "The world will find out sooner or later."

Janus glances at her disapprovingly.

She continues, "Why do you think I hired him at the Blaze and why do you think I invited him to our home? He is the one to tell the story and write your biography too."

Janus grumbles and mumbles under his breath, turning his back to her. He replies, "I'm not ready."

She walks over to him and gently swivels his chair in her direction and says, "I know. But I felt it important for you to meet the man that will introduce your work to the world."

Marguerite kisses Janus on the forehead and walks away.

As time passed, Winston and Raveen made their relationship official. Winston proposed to her during brunch at the South Shore Country Club. The palatial and plush surroundings were the perfect backdrop for the deed. The country club is where the who's who in the Black community spent some of their leisure time.

For the occasion, Winston is certain to have her favorite foods served, and there is a live band that perfectly captures the essence of her favorite crooner, Eric Benet. While the performer belts out "Spend My Life With You," Raveen cries tears of joy as Winston gets down on one knee and proposes.

The good news continues to flow in Winston's life as his inaugural major article is published, bearing the title "The Creation of the Black American Zombie with Zencitravmasi.

His popularity grows day by day, but so does the ire of the powers that be in the fair city of Chicago. Winston begins to feel the same uneasiness that he experienced in Atlanta. He often looks around for the 'White hoodie' guys. He often wonders if the entire trip North is a figment of his and Lori's collective imagination.

He mutters, "Maybe that honey was really LSD? Maybe it was on the glove of that bellhop?" Winston shrugs and tries to clear the entire incident from his mind.

Soon after he does that, the phone rings, it's Marguerite.

Winston answers to hear an unusual excitement in her voice. She asks, "Are you sitting down?"

He humorously pans down his sitting body and then back up, replying, "Yep!"

She continues, "Well... rumor has it that the article you wrote is being considered for a PULITZER!"

Winston leaps out of his chair and dances around his office. His co-workers in the bullpen comically look in his direction. He can hear his name being shouted on the phone.

He stops his celebration to listen to the rest of what she has to say.

Marguerite cautions, "Winston, this is very tentative for obvious reasons."

He asks, "What do you mean?"

She replies, "You, my boy, have opened a proverbial can of worms that requires answers from some pretty important people. When questions get to that level, that means globally, people's pockets will start to be affected."

Winston finishes her thoughts, "And those are the people that approve the awarding of Pulitzers."

Marguerite quickly chimes in, "Exactly! However, the fact that THEY allowed your name to be officially listed is a feat in and of itself. However, I do want to warn you. Stay vigilant, certain individuals will try to take you off the board."

Winston purses his lips, understanding all too well what she means.

She went on, "But don't worry about that right now. Be proud that you have earned a seat at the table. I have to go; Harp and I have an appointment this morning. Have a great day and congratulations again!"

After disconnecting with Marguerite, Winston sits quietly, contemplating all that is happening and everything going on now. Realizing that time is short and that he has to cherish life for what it is, his mind fills with images of his parents, his sister, and his friends, of awards and travels. Amidst these reflections, one face consistently holds its place in the forefront—Raveen.

Months later, Raveen is in bed snuggled under the covers watching the nightly news.

Winston passes by the television and goes to the bathroom. While he does so, the news anchor proceeds to report on a recent story. While the anchor completes that story, a video pops up in the corner of the screen. The video shows police cars and a SWAT team surrounding a building.

The news anchor says, "Now, other stories that have made national news. It has been reported that the body of a Kentucky law enforcement agent was found in the basement of Vernon County Suites. His body was found along with several other unidentified individuals." The camera zooms in on the name of the establishment.

The news anchor continues, "The owner, Vernon Gilbert, was shot to death while police were attempting to take him into custody for questioning. The property is not without its controversy: It was once owned by a well-known Black abolitionist named Hanna-May Gilbert way back when. Researchers say that she is the rumored matriarch and the great-great-great grandmother of the Gilbert family. Hanna-May is said to have gone missing under the strangest of circumstances."

Raveen comments, "Geez...only in America." She changes the channel before Winston enters the room.

He sits on the bed, looks over at her, smiles, and asks, "Are you ready for bed now?"

She responds, "Not quite." Raveen turns to Winston and peels back the blanket, revealing a baby bump.

She rubs her stomach, flashing her diamond wedding ring, and confessing, "You know what I want?"

Winston grins, commenting, "Well, here I am, baby. Ready and willing!"

Raveen playfully rolls her eyes and quips, "Not that, silly. But I'd absolutely adore a pint of chocolate chip ice cream from Swirly's."

Winston, his grin intact, playfully points in the distance, "The one clear across town?"

Raveen responds with a soft, delighted giggle.

Leaning over, Winston plants a gentle kiss on Raveen's lips, then lowers to tenderly kiss her baby bump, saying, "As you wish."

Winston gets out of bed and goes into the walk-in closet.

He puts on his black hoodie and a pair of jeans, commenting, "Keep the bed warm. Be right back."

He leaves and heads for the living room where his wallet and keys are. Although the apartment is dimly lit, glimpses of their meaningful decor can be seen as he passes. The walls are filled with many pieces of black art and photos of him and Raveen together. One of his favorite pieces is a large framed poster of Donny Hathaway, and it reads: "To Be Young, Gifted, and Black."

Winston is just about to go out the front door when his phone rings. He looks at the screen, and it's Detective Parsons.

Winston quickly answers, "Hello."

Parsons replies, "Sorry to call you so late, but I have some bad news." Winston remains silent, and Parsons goes on, "I searched all of the Nora Gales with your great-grandmother's info. I found no one with her specifics. Well, there was one, but she was a white woman who died in 1997."

Winston asks, "Can you send me a photo?"

Parsons replies, "Of course, and I hope you have a good night."

Winston's phone pings.

He opens his text to see an image of a white woman. He quickly scrolls through some images on his phone. He stops on an old scanned photo of his great-grandparents, and the lower portion of the photo shows two names, Wilbur & Nora Gale.

Then he goes back to the photo in the text. The features are eerily similar. He sees his mother in her face. He begins to tear up, mumbling, "Hi, great-grandma!"

Lightly tracing his finger over her image, he brushes away his tears, tucks his phone into his pocket, and then steps out the door.

CHAPTER FIFTEEN

On the way to Swirly's, Winston drives somberly through the quiet streets, his thoughts consumed by his great-grandparent's fate.

He asks himself, "Is my grandfather somewhere under the train tracks, and did my grandmother forget about her family and herself?"

Winston sits at the intersection alone, observing people strolling down the street. A man wears a grin as he films a woman with his cell phone, capturing her striking poses near the corner.

On the opposite side of the street, another couple leisurely makes their way. When the light turns green, Winston slowly pulls off and continues on his way.

All of a sudden, as if from nowhere, a Ford Explorer speeding through the intersection runs the red light, colliding with Winston's car on the right and sending it spinning in a half-circle while causing severe damage.

A crowd swiftly gathers, bystanders pointing and engaged in animated chatter. Winston, still dazed, gingerly emerges from his car, his legs unsteady as he surveys the wreckage.

Amidst the commotion, Winston discerns several concerned voices inquiring, "Are you all right?" Another person urgently calls out, "Has someone called the police?" Yet another offers the advice, "Perhaps you should move your car to prevent another collision."

Still feeling woozy, Winston re-enters the car and attempts to start the engine, but it stubbornly stalls. Sirens wail in the distance, and police lights cast an eerie glow over the scene.

Frustrated and upset, Winston raises his voice, exclaiming, "Look at my car! Look at this!"

The driver of the Explorer is a middle-aged White man, who is clearly intoxicated and leaning out of his driver's side window.

He moans and mumbles, slurring as he says, "Sorry, man... I didn't see you."

Winston shouts out of his now shattered window, "Didn't see me? You ran a red light!"

Two White police officers arrive on the scene. They exit their car and walk straight over to Winston. Winston looks up to see the name tag of the first officer; his name is Handy.

He paces slowly towards Winston with his hand on his gun, yelling, "Sir, stop! Are you trying to flee the scene of an accident?"

Winston can't believe his ears, saying, "Ahhh...no! That guy just hit ME. I'm just trying to move my car out of the street."

Handy stretches his arm out toward Winston as if to tell him to halt.

A crowd starts to gather to watch the scene unfold. The passersby are chattering; it goes from a murmur to a roar.

Handy nods his head to his partner, Panchak, in the direction of the Explorer. Handy barks demands at Winston, "Just stay right here."

Panchak eases toward the Ford Explorer, softly asking the driver, “Sir, can you hear me? Are you okay?”

Intoxicated, the man slurs, “He...he just came out of nowhere.”

Panchak advises, “Sir, don’t move. I think you’re injured.”

He then leans his head into his two-way radio affixed to his bulletproof vest, saying, “Yes, this is badge number 44433.”

Dispatch responds, “Go ahead 44433.”

Panchak continues, “Send a bus to the intersection of South Hyde Park Blvd & E 55th St. The report is: “White middle-aged male injured in a car accident.”

Then he releases the button on the radio.

Dispatch responds, “Bus dispatched.”

Panchak pats the driver on the arm saying, “Sit tight. Paramedics are on the way.”

The driver replies, “Oh God, thank you, Officer. I’m in so much pain.”

Panchak walks away from the Explorer and back toward Officer Handy and Winston but stops near the curb. Panchak motions for Handy, who joins him away from Winston.

He looks at them speaking but is unable to hear them because they are out of his earshot. Winston waits nervously and leans on his car. The officers return together with blank looks in their eyes.

Winston inquires, “Did he tell you that he ran the red light?”

Handy takes a deep breath and informs Winston, “Sir, turn around. You’re under arrest.”

Winston shouts, “Wait... what? He hit me.”

Panchak moves in, jolts Winston around, and begins to handcuff him.

Teary-eyed Winston continues, “You know this shit ain’t right!”

Winston begins to have a full-on panic attack as he watches the police officers and crowd through a warped fish lens. His heart pounds fast while he experiences bright lights and loud noises. The sound of his heartbeat ramps up so loudly, then the noise muffles to complete silence.

Winston hangs his head low while Panchak walks him to the back of the police cruiser.

Panchak opens the door and puts Winston inside.

A member in the crowd shouts, "I saw everything. That White dude in the Explorer hit him. Y'all on some shit!" Another shouts as he records with his cell phone, "Here we go again. Driving While Black. Don't worry fam, I got you. It's all on film."

The intersection has drawn a growing crowd of onlookers, curious about the unfolding scene, which has become all too familiar in their neighborhood. The officers' urgent calls for backup sound nervously through the air, highlighting the rising tensions.

Amidst the commotion, another bystander diverts their attention from Winston's situation to the man inside the Ford Explorer. The driver is apparently sleeping off his intoxication. He's oblivious to the chaos around him, and his loud snores are in sharp contrast with the anxiety he caused at the intersection.

The man recording informs the crowd saying, "This muthafucka' done went to sleep!" The crowd gets louder. He went on, "Wake yo' fat ass up!"

While seated in the back of the police cruiser, Winston can hear the crowd shouting about the police's mistreatment of him and their anger towards the driver. It was a cacophony of support and resentment at the same time.

Winston continues to survey the happenings right outside the window. He wishes that he could take a couple of Zencitravmasi and just make this entire situation go away.

That's when he sees her: a White woman walking her dog, wearing a pair of small-framed dirty eyeglasses. The dog makes eye contact with Winston and begins to ferociously bark at him.

Winston then looks at the lady, and she stares back at him with contempt.

Then she gives him a wicked grin while her dog barks repeatedly at the car. The dog starts to pull his owner in Winston's direction.

Even though he is in the car, Winston feels powerless, like the many Black people before him who had vicious dogs sicced on them by the police. Before they get too close, she pulls the dog back and continues to walk away, but not before she winks at Winston.

Before mayhem can ensue, the officers jump into their cruiser and take Winston to jail. Winston's thoughts drift as the cruiser navigates the streets. He can't help but wonder about the outcome of this ordeal.

He thinks, "Nelivee was right." No matter what he does, justice will never prevail. He could very well be on his way to becoming another statistic in a system that's clearly stacked against people like him.

Winston's phone begins to ring, and then his text messages begin to chime. He knows that it's Raveen wondering what's taking him so long. The officers in the front talk amongst themselves like it's just another day, casually referring to the arrestees like numbers on a bingo card.

Handy said, "All I need is three more this week, and I'll win that weekly bonus!"

Panchak replies, "Dude, it's pretty sweet. I got it last month. An extra two grand is a sweet deal for sweeping darkies off the street!"

All Winston could do was nod his head and pray.

Weeks Later…

Winston sits in the courtroom dressed in a black suit that is somewhat ill-fitted. After the few weeks that he's had, his appetite has suffered right along with him. Winston sits beside his attorney, Angela Samuels, a dazzling Black woman who wears a convincing pretty scowl that advertises that she is not the one to play with. They both occupy the defendant's table which sits before a crowded courtroom.

Winston glances at her and offers a small smile. He isn't necessarily being nice; in this moment, she is the only one who can get him out of this mess he is in. Not to mention, she smells like peaches and fresh-cut flowers, and that is the current highlight of the moment.

Scooting in his chair, he feels an awkward gravitational pull on his left leg. He pans downward, gently raising the hem of his pant leg, and can't help but scoff at the incessantly blinking green light of an ankle monitor.

Angela casts a disapproving glance downward, rolling her eyes in response.

She reassures him, "Don't worry about that ankle monitor. Trust me, it's coming off today."

In a hushed tone, Winston laments, "I shouldn't be wearing this. I shouldn't even be here."

She whispers back with sass, "No one is saying that it's right. Now, let me do my job and correct it."

Winston drops his pant leg and looks around the room. Across from him sit two middle-aged White prosecutors, and behind them is the man who had been driving the Ford Explorer.

There's a familiar voice in the rear of the room. Winston turns around to see a heavily pregnant Raveen toddling into the space and clicking off her cell phone.

A faint, half-hearted smile crosses his face when he sees her. She cradles her swelling belly, her eyes glistening with tears as she returns his smile.

But she isn't the only visitor making an appearance. There they are, Officers Handy and Panchak, donned in full uniform, casting smug glances in his direction. His eyes then meet those of his attorney, who wears a confident and reassuring smile.

She comments, "Don't worry about that either. We've got a dozen witnesses and the traffic cam video. They won't get away with this! Before I forget, I need your license number to complete a file."

She shuffles through some papers while he retrieves his identification.

Winston reaches into his pocket, pulls out his wallet, opens it, and picks through it. That's when he finds the note given to him by the elderly Black man he and Lori had dinner with while on the road.

He opens the note and reads it. It says, "North is South. Don't run, just stand firm. You are never safe!"

Winston cocks his head with a concerned look on his face.

Attorney Samuels gently elbows Winston. In a low voice, she says, "Never mind, it's time."

Winston hurries and pockets the note and his wallet.

From a doorway behind the judge's bench, a bailiff enters the courtroom.

The bailiff continues, "Honorable Judge Nelivee Presiding."

Winston's eyes go wide. He exclaims, "Nelivee?"

His heart begins to race, pounding fast and hard in his chest.

His lawyer looks at him, speaking, but her words seem muted in his ears.

As the judge enters the room, Winston can't help but stare. It isn't just because of his name but also because of the uncanny resemblance to the actor Fred Gwynne, known for playing Herman Munster.

A sense of foreboding washes over Winston; it feels like a bad omen.

Judge Nelivee ascends the stairs to the judge's stand and takes his seat.

After settling in, he opens a file folder filled with documents and begins attempting to read the papers. Suddenly, he starts patting his pockets and searching the desk for something.

He asks, "Where are my damn glasses?"

He opened another desk drawer and commented, "Oh, here they are." He shoved the large black-framed glasses onto his face.

Winston is frozen with fear, noticing that the huge lenses are filthy. They seem to be caked with fingerprints, smears of dirt, and other dried unmentionables.

Winston stares intensely at the murky glasses on the judge's face and tries not to squeal in agony.

Judge Nelivee happily states, "Now, let's get started!"

Winston's heart sinks into his stomach.

His attorney can see that he is in distress. Before she could speak out to implore the judge for a delay or continuance, Judge Nelivee wore a look of disgust on his face, saying, "Bailiff, I can't see out of these god-damn things. Give me something to clean them off."

The Bailiff goes into a small cabinet on the wall and hands the Judge a small spray bottle and a piece of cloth. The judge cleans the glasses and puts them back on his face.

Then he peers at Winston and says, "Mr. Gale, let's see what we can do to get you home."

Tears stream down Winston's face as his attorney holds his hand firmly.

Judge Nelivee not only dropped all charges against him but also reprimanded the officers for their wrongful arrest.

After reviewing the eyewitness videos and the traffic cam footage, the court takes action to press charges against the man who had careened into Winston on that fateful night.

Finally, Winston is liberated to return home to his family and resume his career.

When Winston returns to work, to his surprise, he finds an empty office. No receptionist, no bullpen, or maintenance crew. The further he enters, the more anxious he becomes.

By the time he makes it to his office, expecting the worst, he is shocked yet again. There stands a room full of people. Amongst the group are Marguerite, Dr. Turner, and even Raveen.

Winston asks, "What is this… What's going on?"

Marguerite and Janus pace over to Winston with pride in their eyes. She says, "We had to empty the office for this event."

Winston mutters, "Event?"

Looking over at Raveen, Marguerite says, "We have already shared this with Raveen. She is as important in this as you are. And we needed her to be in a headspace to settle you if it came to that."

Janus comments, "We have something fantastical to tell you."

A man in the group shouts, "All of us here do."

Marguerite goes over and clasps Winston's hand, "Dear boy, everyone here, including you, is the lifeline to a new world."

Winston stutters, "I…I don't understand."

Raveen walks over and takes his other hand, and they both lead him to his desk where he has a seat.

Janus says, "During our interview, you asked me about my research." He then turns and outstretches his arm toward the people lining the back of the room. He goes on, "They are my research."

Winston has a stunned look on his face, and each person begins to speak.

By the end of the night, Winston confides, "I have something to tell you too. It's about my personal migration from Atlanta to Chicago."

Marguerite smiles as this is the story she has been waiting to hear.

Winston takes the floor, and in a hushed, trembling voice, he shares all of the bone-chilling and horrifying details of what happened to him and Lori. Things that until now, he questioned if they were even real. But they were.

Once it's over, Raveen approaches Winston with tears in her eyes, embracing him. The group gradually exits the room, closing the door behind them, and allowing the couple to continue their conversation in private.

Some weeks later…

A diverse and prestigious audience, comprised of influential figures from various fields, sits attentively in the auditorium, their attention focused on the stage. They are gathered for an event aimed at raising awareness of the challenges faced by the African-

American community and fostering stronger alliances to support Black communities.

A woman walks out onto the stage and says, "We have waited all year for this event, and now the time has come. I would like to introduce one of the most esteemed colleagues that I have ever had the pleasure to work with. Without further ado, let's welcome Ms. Raveen Tillson-Gale to the stage!"

The audience claps as Raveen walks out. Winston sits proudly in the audience holding his infant daughter, Nora Raven Gale. Raveen stands confidently behind a podium, proudly peering out into the audience. Her backdrop is adorned with the University of Chicago seal and the logo for the Mayflower Resolution Association.

The room falls into a hushed silence in anticipation of her words. And then, she begins to speak:

"Racism has reached the coveted status of historical preservation. It is lovingly watched over and cared for better than any endangered species one could think of. It speaks volumes that an entire race of people who look like me need to be medicated with pharmaceuticals like "ZENCITRAVMASI" in order to make it through the day.

Because of this targeted oppression, African-American Descendants of the Enslaved suffer from varying Post-Traumatic Stress Disorders. The barbarians at the gate have caused us to suffer undue stress and dysfunctions that are unparalleled. We believe there should be substantial monthly governmental compensation and gains for this persisting condition.

To say that we are under siege is an understatement. We are accosted while we drive, walk down the street, sleep in our homes, swim in pools, and just live life in general. The Damage is extensive. Therefore it is challenging to quantify how a system such as yours can compensate us for not only the taking of our money but our bodies and our time as well.

We require adequate supplementation for a condition that has been forcibly passed down through our ancestors. PTSD is literally in the DNA of African-American people. However, this is only the beginning. There is work that needs to be done in how you see the world regarding Black people. You have made certain that each breath we take culminates in an egregious offense. It seems that no time or place is sufficient for us to be Black. Ultimately, that is what has to change. And it needs to change NOW!"

The End.

The Great Migration was one of the largest movements of people in United States history. Approximately 6 Million Black people moved from the American South to the North and Midwestern states roughly from the 1910s until the 1970s. Millions made the journey, but not everyone arrived.

What happened to them?

About The Author

Yvette Kendall is an accomplished American novelist and screenwriter hailing from the south side of Chicago, Illinois. She is best known for her work as the author of "The GOD Maps, Volume One," the inaugural installment in an enthralling trilogy. Notably, Kendall's distinctive writing style has led her to pioneer a new sub-genre within the realm of science fiction, aptly termed "Biblical Futurism." This innovative genre has succeeded in captivating an entirely fresh audience, drawing them into its uniquely imaginative domain.

In addition to her literary achievements, Yvette Kendall has also made significant strides in the world of screenwriting. She stands as the creative force behind a groundbreaking Social Justice Horror Thriller entitled "NORTH," a project currently in active discussions for adaptation into both a feature film and a television series. However, until then, she has decided to turn those works into literary works. With that said, Kendall was not stopping there, she continued showcasing her genre-defying storytelling prowess in "The Revelation Activation."

However, perhaps the crowning jewel in Yvette Kendall's career is the recent signing of an Option deal, which paves the way for "The GOD Maps" to transition into a mainstream television series bearing the same name. Her prominence in the entertainment industry has expanded her creative footprint into the realm of comic books and graphic novels.

For those eager to delve into her literary works, “The GOD Maps, Volume One” is readily available in a variety of formats, including hardback, paperback, E-Book, and Audiobook, ensuring an enjoyable reading experience for all preferences. Additionally, Yvette Kendall’s bibliography encompasses a diverse range of titles, including “Horrorgraphs and Other Short Creepy Stories,” “IMAGINATION,” and “My Dreams Painted With A.I,”. Kendall also has a host of books for children titled, “A Zombie For Mommy!,” “A Werewolf For Mommy!” (including the French version, “Un Loup-Garou Pour Maman!”), “Delilah Gives SciFi A Try!” (also available in French as “Delilah Essaie SciFi!”), and “Eagan Become a Vegan.”

All of Yvette Kendall’s literary creations are published in collaboration with Stravard Lux Publishing & Distribution Co., a testament to her enduring commitment to delivering captivating narratives to a diverse and ever-expanding audience. For more information visit www.yvettekendall.com

Acknowledgements

I would like to acknowledge everyone who supported my efforts in this piece of work, whether in screenplay, teleplay, or literary formats. I thank you and appreciate your availability at all hours of the day and night. To those who read my work and provided love, encouragement, and EDITING through your critiques, I thank you as well. I understand that I can be challenging to work with when it comes to the quality of my finished product, my vision, and deadlines. In the past, I have been described as 'dogged, relentless, impatient, and militant' on more than one occasion, and these words are absolutely true! And even though not all plans worked out during this process, all of you, in every way, shape, and form, have added value to me as a person and as a writer. You have continued to sow the seeds of improvement into my expanding world of literary.

So, without further ado, I would like to acknowledge the best cheerleaders and feedback Kings and Queens that I know. The award goes to…

Mahari Muhammad, Russ Fulmore, Dawn Burkes, Auriga Cohran, Amandilo Cuzman, Alfonzo Lee Jones, Rain Pryor, David Knoller, Nadine King-Mays, Harold Dennis, Dexter Matthews, Tariq Ali Muhammad, Coco Elysses, Raymond Leonard, Christopher "Slam" Williams, and Marquis "Quis" Simmons.

Credits

Book Formatting: Kimolisa Mings

Book Covers Designed by: Yvette Kendall

Book Publisher: Stravard Lux Publishing & Distribution Co.
www.StravardLux.com

Reviews

"Yvette Kendall is unequivocally the most diabolical and perverted Horror writer ever to come from our community. The story is so enrapturing. It pulls you in yet horrifies you. It's full of suspense and nastiness. It's vulgar while light and humorous. The absolute horror of it all makes me stop and regroup before jumping back in to quell my curiosity. A real page turner. So glad that you have come my way."

~ Auriga Cohran, Chicago, IL.

"NORTH," rendered me speechless. I have never read anything like it, and I found it quite fantastic! Some of the things written in this book, to be honest, are conversations to be had behind closed doors with only family and friends. Yvette Kendall wrote the quiet parts OUT LOUD, and I loved every minute of it. This book needs to be a movie, a TV series, and anything else that will get it to the "Blackity-Black-Black" members of the world. This book is going to spark conversations that will definitely raise some eyebrows."

~ Robert Stevenson, New York, NY.

"It's smart, it's terrifying, and it's thought-provoking. To say that 'NORTH' is unusual is an understatement. I read a review regarding the screenplay of this same title. The reviewer said that 'NORTH' is like a mash-up of 'Get Out' and 'Lovecraft Country.' I'm here to say that is absolutely true! However, 'NORTH' goes a million steps farther."

~ V. Bradley, Los Angeles, CA.

www.ingramcontent.com/pod-product-compliance
Lightning Source LLC
Chambersburg PA
CBHW030412310726
48979CB00002B/383

9781737144076